THE MOTHER OF MY REINVENTION

essays, stories & lyrical assemblages

LORRAINE DEVON WILKE

THE MOTHER OF MY REINVENTION
essays, stories & lyrical assemblages

by Lorraine Devon Wilke

Published in Los Angeles, CA, United States

Print ISBN: 978-0-9964230-5-2
eBook ISBN: 978-0-9964230-4-5
LCCN: 2025924750

This work includes essays, and both fiction and creative non-fiction. In the fictional pieces, all names, characters, businesses, organizations, places, events, and incidents are either products of the author's imagination, used fictitiously, or recreated to protect privacy. Where real-life public names or places appear, the situations, dialogue, and incidents concerning those people and places are fictional and not intended to depict actual events or to change the entirely fictional nature of the work. In all other respects, any resemblance to actual persons, living or dead, or any resemblance to events or locales, are entirely coincidental. The creative non-fiction pieces were written from memory. The author has done her best to be faithful to her experiences.

Cover design by Lorraine Devon Wilke
Cover photograph courtesy of family archives.

Assorted praise for Lorraine Devon Wilke's short works:

"*She Tumbled Down* might be a short story, but it doesn't read like one. The plotting works perfectly and, of course, the beautiful writing is tight, descriptive and keeps you on the edge of your seat from the first sentence."

"Having known Lorraine's many other talents (singing, acting, screenwriting) for a few decades, I'm not at all surprised by the ferocity of this wonderful short story. Achingly real characters, textured prose -- you'll get hooked."

"This is a masterfully told tale, flawlessly written with authentic characters and brimming with drama and reality. A remarkable achievement in the difficult genre of the short story."

"This is powerful stuff. I'm not normally a fan of short stories, rarely read them, but I picked this up because I've previously enjoyed Ms. Wilke's writing style. The writing is precise yet eloquent and the story cleverly plotted, giving you barely a chance to blink. Thought-provoking and emotive. Highly recommended."

"Authors like you are the reason readers keep falling in love with books. It takes vision, courage, and persistence to bring a story like that into the world. That's something truly worth commending."

"Beautifully written essay - and much appreciated. Thanks for laying this out so well. I'm sharing you and your words with all our family, those in the US and those abroad."

"A breath of fresh air in this crazy world! Thanks for posting and for your ever-inspired prose!"

"This story is so vivid, filled with real human beings whose lives are turned upside down and inside out in a split second -- just the way such moments can happen to any of us."

NOVELS BY LORRAINE DEVON WILKE

After the Sucker Punch

Hysterical Love

The Alchemy of Noise

Chick Singer

To everyone who inspired what's inside.

TABLE OF CONTENTS

WHAT BROUGHT THIS ON ...

Writing a novel is a journey. You're struck by, or stumble upon, an idea that requires many words to be amply told, and moved by that idea, you set off to find those words. You follow the characters—their thoughts, dreams, actions; *their* words—pulled forward, always, by the unfolding narrative that carries you through to "The End." It's a powerful and invigorating process, one I've now done, and loved doing, several times.

But I've also written smaller things with fewer words, and after recently completing a short story I liked a lot, I got to thinking it might be refreshing to share some of my other, less voluminous, works with people who've read my novels, who follow me on my various online platforms, and just might enjoy a compilation of smaller things.

So I've pulled together some of my favorite short stories, select essays, and an assemblage of lyrics (with links to their recorded tracks) with the hope that you'll be entertained, moved, provoked, and interested; that you'll listen to some music, have an emotional experience, a little cry maybe, even a laugh or two. Certainly that's my goal with this: sharing words that make you *feel* something in reading them.

Thank you for picking up this book. I'm always grateful for your interest in my words, the many or the few, and hope you enjoy the read.

~ Lorraine

PENELOPE FOR HIS THOUGHTS

a short story

HE HADN'T NOTICED the depth of his malaise, the sheer agony and grasp of it, until dawn rose that particular day. The day when his low-grade fever of boredom—expected response to retirement after decades of gainful, if uninspired, employment—slipped into despair.

Almost nine-and-a-half months after packing up his desk at Mid-Town Auto Parts & Smog Tests of Murphysboro, Illinois, he felt the exact moment, around 7:04 a.m., when whatever life force remained in his depleted, diminished self slowly seeped out like the last gasp of a withered balloon, rendering him empty. Bereft of anything even resembling life force. He could do nothing but slump in his worn recliner and note the sag of his soul.

With a deep, guttural sigh, he picked up his book—the tenth-in-a-series of interchangeable spy yarns committee-written under a famous author's name—and commenced reading with dulled inattention.

Roland Caine was sixty-nine-years-old, an old sixty-nine at a time when even that age dangled the option of vitality. Not for Roland. He had little interest in vitality. Its required dedication to health, fitness, and personal composition was too exhausting to consider. He didn't want to work that hard. He'd already worked harder than he ever wanted to again. He felt old, he saw himself as old, so he accepted his agedness with weary abdication.

For him this entailed painful knees and an oversized gut; scalp-crust behind both ears, and the total absence of sartorial vanity. He seldom combed his remaining strands, allowing them to stick haphazardly to his bald, greasy pate, and found changing clothes to be pointless, sleeping in the same sweatpants and flannel shirt for days on end. Though he regularly watched the five o'clock news with his wife, Connie, their only predictable time together, he had little interest in politics and felt no responsibility to have an opinion. About anything. Even sports bored him.

"You're depressed," Connie announced upon entering the den to find him in the exact position he'd been in when she left for yoga. He may have moved at some point, surely to use the bathroom or grab the sandwich she'd left in the fridge, but it was also possible he hadn't. The room was dark, redolent with Roland's sour smell. Connie flung the curtains back and slid the window open. "It reeks in here." She waved her hands around as if escorting Roland's odor to the outside world.

He ignored her.

"Did you eat?" she asked sharply. "I left a ham and cheese in the—"

"I ate. Thank you." He stayed focused on his book, annoyed that the interruption had him re-reading an inane passage about a big-busted counterintelligence officer who was inexplicably naked in almost every scene in which she appeared. This sort of silliness used to thrill Roland, stir his libido in ways his wife hadn't for years, but now it did nothing but confirm the idiocy of gratuitous literary sex.

Connie plunked down on the arm of the sofa, eyebrows pinched, and pondered Roland's state. As an active sixty-five-year-old who'd stayed current and kept fit even while raising two girls and wrangling a career in food distribution (high schools, colleges, prisons), Connie was once again struck by her miscalculation. She'd presumed, as wives often do, that Roland's retirement would inspire a resurgence of shared activity: increased travel, more frequent dinner parties, extended time with the grandkids; certainly an uptick in the intimacy sadly lacking in recent years. Instead, as she bloomed, he faded. As she embraced her own retirement (commenced shortly after his), he shrank into the gray of obsolescence. It left her deeply resentful, but all she could say was: "You need to change that shirt. I can smell it from here."

He looked up and nodded, then went back to the naked spy.

At one o'clock in the afternoon, napping for the second time that day, Roland was startled awake when Connie burst back into the den, tittering with excitement. "There's a peacock in our front yard!"

He adjusted the chair to an upright position. "A peacock? That can't be right."

"Well, it's out there. I just stood watching it for the last five minutes. It's got the little green crown, the whole thing."

He pushed himself out of the chair and walked to the window, looked out over the early-summer lawn, rough and sprouting. "There's nothing out there."

She dashed from the room, calling out from the front door, "Oh my goodness, Roland; it's up on the porch now!" The pitch in her voice was infectious; Roland felt a surprising jolt of energy. He slipped on his moccasins and, at a faster clip than usual, walked to the foyer.

Connie stood with the door cracked, eyes sparkling. "Look," she whispered. "It's still out there, just feet from the door. I'll go get something; maybe it's hungry."

As she rushed to the kitchen, Roland crept up to the door and peeked out.

There it was. A large, completely incongruous wild bird shuffling around the porch, nibbling whatever seeded things were retrievable from between the slats.

"It's a peahen," he corrected Connie when she returned with a bowl of crumbled Triscuits. "It doesn't have the big, feathered tail like the male; that's the peacock. She's the female."

"Oh, I see," Connie, delighted to have something, anything, to talk to her husband about besides the weather, leaned in closely. "Is she still out there?"

He opened the door wider, and they both peered out. The peahen was strutting around their large wooden porch as if it were territory well known. Roland took the bowl from Connie's hand and stepped cautiously from the foyer. As the hen focused on a small planter near the steps several feet away, Roland slid into a porch chair by the door and sprinkled a handful of cracker crumbs in a semi-circle around his feet.

He waited.

Connie waited.

After a good long minute, the hen finally took notice of Roland's offerings, and intrigued by the unexpected bounty, inched closer with each peck. Roland found himself oddly anticipatory of her approach, pleased, in a way, that his presence wasn't judged an obstacle to her task. When she was within inches, he leaned down and placed a piece of cracker on the toe of his moccasin.

Connie shook her head, whispering, "Oh, she's not going to—"

The hen snatched the cracker from his foot and stood there, munching, looking around as birds are wont to do, until it finally glanced up at Roland. For a nanosecond he was convinced their eyes held.

"Well, how about that?" Connie chortled. "No fear at all. Let me try." She leaned through the door, grabbed a few bits from the bowl, and held out her hand. The bird, with neither a move nor glance in Connie's direction, turned and sashayed down the steps.

"Well, guess *I* don't rate." She laughed. "Or maybe you're just the bird whisperer."

Roland flushed at the comment. Which was odd, since it really meant nothing. But he liked that he hadn't scared the bird off; that she'd chosen him over his wife. He liked that Connie noticed and framed it as such. It made him feel special. Dogs and cats like anyone, but a peahen? That didn't happen every day.

As the bird made her way across the street, through another yard, and off to parts unknown, Connie looked at Roland wistfully. "That was unique. Wonder where she came from?"

"She must've broken out of an enclosure or something. Probably lives in that wetland area behind the school. Maybe she's one of their pet projects, who knows? Anyway, odds are good we'll never see her again."

He stood and flexed his aching knees. The excitement was over. He headed back to his book and his boredom.

The next morning Roland settled into the den at 7:30 a.m., and though wide-awake when he got there, was sound asleep within thirty minutes. Three hours later, the abrupt scraping of the window being thrown open snapped him from slumber.

"I swear to God, Roland, it smells like a compost heap in here!" Connie's face conveyed authentic disgust. "I never thought I'd say this to my own husband, but if you insist on living like a bum, I'd prefer you take it to the basement."

She wasn't kidding; that was clear.

He didn't appreciate her assaultive approach. He adjusted the chair until he was sitting up. He set his book aside and huffed with indignation. "If a man can't be comfortable in his own home, what the hell's the point?"

"The point, Roland, is that you have to find a way to be comfortable without behaving like a hobo. I work too hard making this home a lovely place to have you turn it into a freeway underpass."

She swept out to the kitchen to quickly return with a plate of food and a can of soda pop. "It's practically lunchtime so I made you a tuna with egg, your favorite; here's a bag of Ruffles, also your favorite, and I got cream sodas yesterday, your third favorite." She set everything down at his side table, then set herself down on the couch. "I'm doing everything I can to cheer you up, Roland, but if you're uncheerable, there's nothing more I *can* do. I'm going on with my life regardless."

"What does that mean?" he asked with genuine alarm.

"I've planned several short trips with friends, sightseeing kinds of things, and I'm taking a photography class at the university. I've always wanted to take better pictures. I'd hoped we'd be doing some of these things together, but I guess not." She stood up, brushed her hands on her slacks, and straightened her hair. "I'm headed to Carbondale right now. Afterwards I'm going to a movie and dinner with some of the girls, so I'll see you later."

When she got to the door, she stopped and looked back. "Please take a shower today, maybe walk around the block. Pretend you're alive for a minute or two. If nothing else it'll get your blood moving." Her head tilted with a sad smile and then she was gone.

Roland sat in a state of incomprehension. Photography? She'd never expressed one iota of interest in photography; how was he to know it was something she wanted to do? He found himself irritated, thinking about the years of hard work he'd put in to afford this home she'd just accused him of sullying.

Then, of course, he remembered that her job paid nearly as much as his and provided the excellent health insurance they'd had throughout the years. He could hardly claim superiority on those grounds. He sighed again. There was no winning.

He briefly considered her admonition to take a walk. Maybe he should. These were still the cooler days of early summer, and if he was going to take a shower, may as well work up a bit of a sweat first. He'd at least feel like he'd accomplished something.

Then he thought about getting his shoes on, finding the right hat; deciding which blocks to take to avoid which neighbors, and it all became too much.

He leaned back in his chair and was overcome by his loss of happiness. He'd never been a particularly jolly fellow, but he'd had *some* happiness, surely. Now he had none, nothing to be happy about: no job, no projects, no goals or aspirations; no deadlines, nothing anyone expected of him; nothing to do other than mindlessly walk and read banal books.

He didn't even like his grandkids at the moment. They were exceedingly messy, far too loud, and relentlessly in motion. He certainly loved his two daughters, but they were obsessive parent-types who felt everything about their children was noteworthy; their expectations of him to feel the same were oppressive. He tended to avoid them lately. The only thing he liked right now was Connie and she didn't like him.

He closed his eyes and fell into the blackness of his gloom. It was a deep, dark place that appeared to have no bottom, and there was comfort in letting himself be swallowed up, farther and farther down until—

Tap-tap-tap.

A peculiar noise hit his eardrums. Another sharp *tap*, then a scratching sound. At first he thought he'd imagined it, but there it was again. He raised the chair and got up, flushed with inexplicable anticipation. He rushed to the front door and slowly, quietly, opened it a crack.

There she stood … the peahen.

She looked up at him as if she'd been waiting and was a tad annoyed. He smiled. "Hello there!"

Amidst subtle clucks of salutation, she immediately turned and began strutting around the porch, head jutting back occasionally as if inviting him to join her.

His breath quickened. This was no accident, no coincidence. It couldn't be. Peahens don't come to your door every day. If they do appear by chance, there can be no denying a second visit is by choice.

Roland hurried to the kitchen for something to share with his visitor. A small bag of sunflower seeds sat on the counter—clearly one of Connie's "healthy snacks." Whatever hesitation he felt about co-opting her provisions was lost in the urgency to quickly get back.

Ah! Still there, still clucking around the flowerpots to the left of the stairs, seemingly in no hurry to rush off. Roland stepped quietly out to the porch, and sat, once again, in the chair by the door, scattering sunflower seeds around his feet.

He waited. She ignored him. He tapped his toe. She ignored him. He whistled softly. She ignored him. Then, as if deciding she'd toyed with him long enough, she purposefully made her way to the treats and dove in.

Roland was charmed by her enthusiasm. "Better than that fertilizer stuff, isn't it?" He piled a few seeds on the toe of his moccasin, and she didn't disappoint, striding close enough for him to touch. When he reached out ever so cautiously, his palm stacked with seeds, she balked only seconds before pecking right from his hand.

He felt triumphant. Which was ridiculous, he knew, but given the dearth of uplift lately, he was tickled by her proximity. As she stretched her long neck for the last morsel, she briefly brushed against his hand. He noted the softness of her feathers. In a quick turn, she strutted away, down the steps, across the yard and off to wherever it was she went.

He took a deep breath and felt … something. He couldn't say what, but it held some harmonic of positive emotion. Which was absurd, really. But he felt it, nonetheless.

Penelope, he thought. I'll call her Penelope. He'd always liked the sound of that name but had never known a woman who bore it. It perfectly fit his new friend. Penelope the Peahen.

He would keep that to himself, naming her. Connie would find it silly. But he didn't care. It made him happy.

Connie was stunned to walk into the den at ten o'clock the following morning to find Roland showered, shaved, and in clean clothes. She stopped and stared without a word, but he didn't look up from his book, aware that his status would be surprising and reluctant to make a fuss about it.

"Do you have a doctor appointment today?" she finally asked.

"What?" He looked up as if just noticing her.

"Do you have a doctor appointment I forgot about?"

"No. Why?"

"Just wondered." She began picking up random items from

around the room, pretending there was nothing unusual at hand. "You look like you're ready to go out."

He watched her and felt a stab of affection. "No. I just decided you had a point, and I didn't want you to have to keep making it."

She couldn't tell if the comment was snide or conciliatory. When he gave her a wan smile she decided to go with the latter. "Well … good. I appreciate that."

"I thought you might." He seemed genuine.

"Did you eat?"

"I had a bowl of cereal."

"Have you got anything going on this afternoon?" It was a ludicrous question, as they both knew, but it was her habit to ask.

"Just here. How about you?"

"I start my class today. It's a pretty intense schedule: twelve to three, five days a week for two weeks, so I'll be—"

"I hope you enjoy it." He went back to reading.

She looked at him warily, his behavior incongruous enough to be noted. "I'm sure I will." She picked up his cereal bowl from the side table. "Okay then … I'm going to yoga and then onto class, so I'll see you later this evening."

He glanced up from his book. "Yes. See you tonight."

She leaned in and kissed the top of his clean head. They so seldom touched these days it surprised him. He patted her cheek before she swept off.

As soon as he heard the front door click shut, he got up and rushed to the kitchen. From the lower cabinet where baking bowls and other seldom-used items were stashed, he retrieved the supplies he'd purchased from the corner market hours earlier: sunflower and sesame seeds, currants, and packs of various crackers. He pulled a cereal bowl from the shelf and filled it with a mix of everything he had, then tucked the bags back behind the Cuisinart. He went out to the front porch and settled in his usual chair.

To wait.

For Penelope.

The street was quiet, traffic minimal, and he found himself enjoying the coolness of the early summer morning. He scattered the treats around his feet in typical fashion and leaned back to await his expected guest.

Glancing around at the houses that shared the street with them, Roland thought about the various people living in those abodes. Directly across were the Fairfields. They used to come over for barbeques on occasion, but with several kids now distributed at colleges around the country, they were seldom available. To the left of them were the Cutters, Mike and Sandy. They'd initially been frequent guests at the Caine household, but after too many Trivial Pursuit nights in which Mike's rabid competitiveness got aggressive, Roland decided the guy was an asshole.

There were others with whom they'd done this or that, but it was a different time now, different in this post-Covid era. That the neighborhood remained a decent place was good enough. That people kept largely to themselves these days was his preference.

As if summoned by Roland's musings, Mike Cutter pulled from his garage and out to the street. When he noticed Roland on the porch, he stopped, opened the window and leaned out. "Hey there, Roland, haven't seen you in a while. How's retirement going?"

"Just fine." Roland nodded.

"Wish I could join you on that porch, but I gotta get going. Be careful, buddy; looks like you've packed on a few. Retirement will do that to ya!" He snorted and patted his relatively flat stomach, taking off with a wave.

"Asshole," Roland muttered.

Face hot with annoyance, hands clasped over his remarked-upon girth, he decided he wouldn't let Mike sour the morning. It was too nice a day and he had a guest to look forward to. He closed his eyes and drifted off.

At two-thirty, he jolted awake, stunned to realize he'd napped for so long. He quickly looked around. She hadn't come. Nothing had been disturbed on the porch except for the few seeds scattered by fluttering sparrows.

His disappointment was palpable. Both Penelope's previous visits had been around one o'clock; it had been reasonable to expect the same today. At two-thirty, it was reasonable to assume otherwise.

He felt the tugging urge to cry, which he knew was irrational. But he'd been so anticipatory of her visit it never occurred to him it was just as likely he'd never see her again, considering he'd never seen her prior.

How strange I am, he thought to himself. He and Connie had never even owned a pet, and now he was mopey about a peahen?

Hungry, he snacked from Penelope's bowl and before long was once again slouched in sleep.

"OUCH!"

Yanked from rumbling dreams by a sharp pain in his toe, Roland awoke to find Penelope at his feet, happily imbibing in the scattered feast. He had no idea how long he'd been out this time, but in a rush of elation he sat up, careful not to spook her. She clucked and flounced and ate and strutted, and he had the distinct feeling it was all for his benefit.

"So, Miss Penelope," he whispered with a smile, "I guess you weren't ready to ditch old Roland after all."

He felt warm and chosen.

He reached out his hand, filled with seeds and, again, Penelope got close enough to peck leisurely from his palm. Roland attempted to run his other hand down her feathered back, but she would have none of that, skittering away.

"Okay, okay," he laughed, "too soon. I get it."

With a coy glance back in his direction, she hopped down the stairs and across the lawn.

"Glad you enjoyed the meal," he called out. "See you

tomorrow!" She crossed the street, slowly disappearing from view.

Roland, energized by their brief encounter, went inside and did something he hadn't done in nearly a year: he made a pot of spaghetti sauce for dinner. To say Connie was surprised later would be an understatement.

Though it was impossible to predict how long Penelope might continue her visitations, Roland decided to up the odds by providing irresistible grub to keep her enticed. He spent time in the local market scouring shelves for new seeds, new nuts, and different crackers, and every day that week, usually around one o'clock in the afternoon, Penelope did him the honor of stopping by for a shared meal. Roland considered it the peak of his social life. Which, of course, it was.

While Connie was off learning about apertures and depth of field, taking in movies and sharing dinners with friends, Roland begged off every invitation with claims of disinterest or lack of energy. He went nowhere and did nothing, so Connie had finally stopped asking. Now she couldn't help but notice the change in his demeanor.

Without prompting—something she'd grown weary of over the months—he'd showered and shaved daily this week, sporting clean clothes as a matter of routine. She also detected a subtle skip to his step whenever he traversed the house, which stymied her. Given that he didn't appear to be getting any exercise and didn't seem to have any friends or neighbors occupying his time and attention, the mood shift was confounding.

"Roland." She sat down on the den couch. "Can I talk to you?"

He put his book down and looked up. "Sure." There was no irritation in his face. That, too, was odd. He typically got peevish when she interrupted his reading.

"I'm taking off tomorrow for a field trip with the girls. We're driving up to Springfield to do the Lincoln tour I've always wanted to do."

His first thought was that he'd had no idea she wanted to do the Lincoln tour. The second was that it was a good long drive.

"That's a good, long drive," he said, echoing his second thought.

"Just a bit over 600 miles, and four of us are going. We'll take turns driving, and we're giving ourselves a whole day to get there. The tour is scheduled for Saturday. Class was cancelled on Monday, so I won't be back until that night. Now, I've left some prepared meals and—"

"I'll be fine, Connie. Just go have a good time."

His words were like a foreign tongue. She'd expected him to grumble about having to warm up his food, or being alone for four days, or not knowing where she kept this or that; his benevolence was disorienting.

"Thank you, Roland," she said hesitantly, "I will." She also knew she'd be giving some hard thought to this new husband who'd emerged in recent days.

But for Roland her outing was a reprieve. He'd been wondering how to juggle the weekend; how to be available for Penelope without getting Connie too involved. It wasn't that she wouldn't appreciate seeing the bird again, and it wasn't that Roland minded if she shared her visits. It was that he feared she'd see just how attached he'd become and judge him ridiculous. Think him crazy. Decide he'd finally lost his marbles.

He didn't want any suggestions of that nature to be triggered. Nor did he want to explain himself. He knew his enthusiasm tipped the scales a bit—naming her might seem eccentric to his wife—but he wasn't obsessed, surely. Not like those Tokyo businessmen with their life-sized "love dolls," or people who let their dogs lick their mouths. Now *that* was too much.

He was just a regular guy who got a kick out of a wild peahen who seemed to get a kick out of him. He looked forward to the connection. He felt honored by her attraction to him and his snacks… and he *was* aware the snacks were the hook; he wasn't that delusional.

So while Connie packed her weekend bag upstairs, Roland quietly prepped three bowls of seeds and crackers for the days ahead, eager to be able to just sit back, relax, and enjoy the time. He hummed as he wrapped Saran around each bowl and tucked them into the lower cabinet. He cleaned the counter, wiped his hands, and smiled. Both he and Connie were going to have really nice weekends.

But he did not.

Penelope never came. Not once. Not Friday, not Saturday, not Sunday. She was a complete no-show.

He was gut sick. So frantic by Sunday night, he eschewed the five o'clock news to roam the neighborhood in hopes of finding her, irked when Mike Cutter, out mowing his lawn in the remaining light of day, came on like an ambush.

"Well, howdy, Roland. Twice in one week, that's gotta be a record," he grinned.

Roland barely slowed his step. Without bothering to make eye contact, he gave a quick, "Hi, Mike," and kept walking.

"Hey!" Mike quickly turned off the mower and moved to the fence. "Roland, hang on."

Roland reluctantly stopped. "What's up?"

"I feel like we haven't been very neighborly lately, what with everyone keeping to themselves after this damn pandemic. How are things going over there?"

"Fine. Connie's busy with all her stuff and the kids, and I'm enjoying my retirement, like you said."

Mike laughed. "Lucky guy! I still got five more years but let me tell ya; the minute I hand in those keys, I set sail for the world and won't be back till I've seen the whole damn thing!"

Mike never failed to make clear he was younger, which irritated Roland, but there was likely another dig in there as well. Being the observant sort he was, Mike had to have noticed Roland and Connie didn't get out much.

Sail the world. Asshole.

Then Roland was struck by a thought: there might be some value in chatting up a guy who spent more time observing the neighborhood than he did. "Say, Mike, this might be a silly question, but have you seen a peahen around here lately, just wandering around the neighborhood?" He tried to keep the question as casual as he could.

"Hell, yes, I've seen that damn thing! Sandy found it ripping up her garden a few weeks ago so now we gotta make sure the gate's always latched, which is a pain in the ass."

"Yeah, they can be … feisty!" Roland felt immediately defensive but kept smiling. "Any idea where she came from?"

"Nah. Some idiot probably got it as a chick, threw it out when it got too big for the cage. All I know is, Sandy'll beat its head in with a shovel if it gets anywhere near her garden again … peahen stew all around!" he guffawed.

Roland clenched his fist, tamping a sharp impulse to smash Mike's stupid face in. "Okay, well—"

"Why do you ask?"

"No big deal. It's just been up on my porch a few times … kind of a hoot. Haven't seen it lately though."

"To each his own, buddy. It comes over here, it's stew."

Roland clenched again and, with a terse nod, hurried off. One more spin around the neighborhood and he headed home, bereft.

By Monday evening and no Penelope, Roland moved beyond grief to metastasizing anger. Mike's cavalier threats openly suggested that neither he nor his wife would have any compunction about beating a living creature to death, and that was a vile prospect. Roland's stomach knotted just thinking about it.

Connie was due home that night, giving him the distraction of cleaning the kitchen—which he'd allowed to sink into disarray—as well as get upstairs for a shower and shave. The last thing he needed was her questioning his regression to old behaviors.

But as he soaped and scrubbed his anxiety sweat and the dirt between his toes from forays around the neighborhood, his rage boiled unabated. He was not going to be passive about Penelope's imminent danger; it was absurd to think he would. He owed as much to that benign little being whose only sin was being true to her nature.

He knew the gate to the Cutter's backyard had just a typical drop latch and was easy to open. A late-night visit to check trash bins and compost heaps was warranted; he had to be sure they hadn't already disposed of her. Not tonight, what with Connie arriving home, but if Penelope hadn't shown by tomorrow, his mission was fated.

Connie's homecoming was pleasant; she'd been animated while filling him in on the trip, but when she hadn't come into the den by ten o'clock the following morning, Roland was concerned enough to climb out of his recliner to go find her.

She was seated at the dining room table, face pale, lips dry, her eyes red and swollen. She didn't look up when he walked into the room.

"What's wrong?" Roland was suddenly terrified that something unexpected had happened to his beloved, if ignored, wife. She looked at him with such anguish his heart jumped. "What is it? What's going on? Are you—"

"Who's Penelope?"

It hit like a blow to the chest. "Penelope?" he queried weakly.

"Yes. Penelope."

"Oh, um—"

"I'd been wondering what was behind your sudden change in hygiene, your uplifted mood, your unusual perkiness lately. I didn't want to be the suspicious wife, particularly since I couldn't imagine how you could possibly have met anyone given your general state of agoraphobia. But then last night I was awakened by you thrashing around the bed mumbling 'Penelope' over and over, and there seemed little doubt. Be honest with me, Roland … are you having an affair?"

"Good lord!" It was so absurd he almost laughed.

"Even an emotional one … or online … through a porn site or with some phone sex operator? Or have you actually met someone?"

By now tears were streaming down her face and Roland felt, quite possibly, like the worst husband in the world. He went to her and put his arms around her in the first embrace he'd offered in months. She stiffened, but he blurted out his explanation:

"No, no, oh, my God, no … there's no woman. No woman at all. Penelope is the peahen."

Her reaction was so abrupt she flung his arms away from her body. "The *peahen*? The *pea*hen?" she shrieked. "What in the crazy hell are you talking about, Roland?"

"It is crazy, I know, but yes, it's the peahen … I gave her the name Penelope, just something silly to call her … because she's been visiting in the afternoons quite a bit."

He was so frantic to assuage Connie's fears he forgot how deranged he might sound. Which clearly he did, given the look on her face. He continued, nonetheless.

"She came around so regularly I started making these little bowls of seeds and stuff, and every day she came, around one o'clock, she'd come right up to me and eat from my hand. I even felt her neck one time; she was that close. And it seemed like she remembered me, you know, like she came specifically to see me. The 'bird whisperer,' like you said, right? So I got used to it, I looked forward to it. Then over the weekend she stopped coming. It's like she disappeared. It was so strange I went looking for her around the neighborhood but no luck. I even talked to Mike Cutter, but he got all weird about her eating up their garden or something, and I honestly suspect he might have done something to her, even killed her. He said Sandy might—"

"ROLAND!" Connie snapped. "SHUT UP! You sound like an absolute lunatic."

He did.

She looked at him fiercely. "Why on earth would you be rolling around in bed calling out the name of a peahen? Do you know how insane that sounds?"

He did. It sounded completely insane. "But you have to understand, Con: she visited me every day, and then all of a sudden, poof, she's gone. Wouldn't you worry if someone you cared about just disappeared like that?" Beyond tempering his anxiety, he felt tears building.

Now it was Connie's turn to consider him with solicitude, adjusting her tone. "Oh, Roland," she said softly. "You need to see a therapist, sweetheart. You really do." She stood up, dried her eyes and rearranged her face, swinging swiftly from injured wife to concerned spouse. She patted his head tenderly. "I'm going to call your doctor and see if he can recommend someone. I think if you can just talk about what you've been going through since your retirement—your loneliness, your isolation, your sense of irrelevance—it will go a long way toward alleviating your transference issues with this poor little peahen."

Before Roland could react or respond, she marched off on her mission, unwilling to give him a moment to debate the prescription.

He, of course, knew she was wrong. He did not need to speak to a therapist. He needed to find Penelope.

But, once again, she didn't come.

So later that night, as Connie snored softly in the bed beside him, Roland got up, slipped on his walking shoes and snuck cautiously from the bedroom. Downstairs, he grabbed his camouflage hunting jacket and pulled a brimmed cap down to his eyebrows. The front door had a persistent squeak, so he tiptoed to the kitchen, picked up a flashlight, and made his way out the back.

It was late enough, dark enough, to support clandestine maneuvers, but luckily the moon offered sufficient illumination to find his way to the Cutter's backyard gate. With shallow breath and heart beating like timpani, he was rewarded with a well-oiled latch. Opening it without a sound, he slid through the gate to their fastidiously landscaped backyard.

His hands were shaking and sweat rolled down his back. After perusing the garden—nary a stalk out of place—he moved to the shed in the southwest corner. He was convinced if any remains remained, they'd be in there, at least until garbage day, a thought that almost made him choke on his strangled breath.

When he got to the shed, he tested the door. Again, no lock, just another drop latch, which he opened with ease. He found a small planter near the entrance to prop the door open, concerned the beam of his flashlight might be seen through the windows.

Three garbage bins were lined to his right. He lifted the green lid and, with the handle of a broomstick, rustled through the branches and leaves to see if anything more solid was contained. Didn't seem to be. He decided to forego the recycling bin; there was little likelihood they'd have thrown her body in there. But the trash container stood full and ominous. It might take him some time, but he was determined to get to the bottom of it.

Just as he angled to pull up the lid, a creak at the door startled him. His breath caught, but before he could turn, the barrel of a shotgun was shoved into his back.

"Move the fuck away from those bins," Mike growled, "or I'll blow your fucking head off." His voice sounded like gravel and razor blades.

Roland could have simply said, "Mike, it's me, Roland!" or put his hands up and pivoted so Mike could see his face, but for some inexplicable reason, and without a whit of wisdom or forethought, he was seized by a burst of combustible anger. In that perilous moment, he just *knew* this heinous man had killed his bird, he *knew* her shattered body had been discarded like so much trash, and he *knew* he was going to kick the living shit out of his arrogant, asshole neighbor.

With a roar that might have wakened the entire neighborhood, Roland swung around with little regard for the firearm at his back and came at Mike like a frenzied bear. Mike was so startled to see his former Trivial Pursuit opponent coming at him with teeth bared, eyes flashing, and rage propelling the charge, he stepped back, lost his footing, and crashed through the door of the shed to the lawn outside. Roland leapt on top of him, arms flailing and fists pummeling with clear intent to inflict damage.

"You motherfucking murderer!!" Roland bellowed. "WHERE IS SHE? What did you do with her?"

Blood spurt from Mike's shattered nose, but even as he attempted to flip his body to a more defensive position, he was helpless in the flurry of blows. The back porch light flipped on. Sandy came flying down the stairs, hair streaming, her mouth wide in a scream.

"ROLAND CAINE, GET OFF MY HUSBAND RIGHT NOW! I've called your wife, I've called the police, and they'll be here in minutes. GET OFF HIM NOW or I promise I will use that shotgun!!"

But Roland heard nothing. Every ounce of his anger, his disappointment, rage, sorrow, loneliness, heartache, fear, and longing was driving this onslaught. He had no control. His nose ran, his tears streamed; his anguish was raw and primal, and all Mike could do was cover his head in hopes of mitigating further injury.

"ROLAND!" Connie's piercing shriek suddenly reverberated like a loudspeaker. Even in the din of his internal chaos, Roland heard her. It shocked him. Connie? What was she doing here?

His mind went blank, and he stopped moving, stopped howling, stopped flailing on his bloodied neighbor, and fell back on the lawn. Within moments, the just-arrived police swarmed on top of him, shouting commands and pinning him motionless, while Sandy administered to her battered husband and Connie stood in horrified silence.

As rights were read, handcuffs applied, first aid rendered, and order restored, Roland's eyes averted just long enough to see, in a moment of surreal irony, Penelope, strutting down the quiet street, blissfully unaware of all that had just transpired on her behalf.

One doesn't necessarily recover from a psychotic event of such magnitude. They simply get past it; hopefully heal the mental lesions that led to it and gratefully accept the forgiveness and compassion of those who love them. That was Roland's assignment.

Initially Mike was unyielding in his intent to pursue aggravated assault charges; certainly the prosecutor was on board. But as wounds healed, and time was spent talking to both Connie and Sandy, gaining empathy for an "old guy who lost his mind in post-retirement depression" (as Connie had so bluntly put it), he ultimately agreed to Roland's plea of "simple battery misdemeanor," which came with a $2500 fine, two years' probation, no jail time, but the mandate of talk therapy and pharmaceutical intervention for at least one full year. He was also required to pay Mike's related medical bills and refrain from proximity to the Cutters or their property.

Despite what had been settled legally, however, on a personal level, Sandy and Mike, along with several other neighbors, retreated behind an untraversable wall of sequestration. Connie felt deep embarrassment at their new role as the neighborhood pariahs, but her priority was getting Roland healthy and rebuilding their life together. Over time, she presumed the neighbors would move on to other gossip-worthy matters.

Lastly, on advice from her own therapist, she got Roland a cat. A sweet animal of gentle demeanor who seemed as devoted to Roland as he was to her. It was a good remedy. It didn't demand the engagement of a dog—having to walk neighborhood streets was certainly *not* a good idea at this juncture—but did offer him companionship and attachment. He named her Lily.

They screened in the front porch so Roland could enjoy that space without fear of Lily bolting, and he was often out there, even on cold days, sipping his coffee, cuddling her on his lap, watching as life went by on a street that no longer felt like his own. He'd occasionally see Mike or Sandy emerge from their house or garage and, whenever he did, a pang of remorse was felt.

There was one time when he thought he saw Penelope strutting between the houses a few doors down from the Cutter's, but he was probably imagining it.

The End

Inspired by a peahen who, for many months, made pilgrimages to our front yard for Triscuit crumbs and attention from my husband (who is most certainly not *a "Roland"!), "Penelope for His Thoughts" was awarded by Tulip Tree Publishing and included in their anthology,* Stories That Need To Be Told, 2019.

Photo by LDW

MY SEARCH FOR YOU

song for a father

You were puzzled by my need for clarity
Maybe you thought I depended on language too much
But there were volumes you didn't say or I never heard
I know you thought the way you loved was surely enough

So elusive, I wonder if you ever figured out
How your silence always made me feel a little loud?
So convinced if I sang and danced and jumped up and down
You would see me, just me, and maybe be a little proud

And sometimes I know that you heard me
Sometimes I know that you cried

CHORUS
But you left me in early December
You loved me but we both knew our time was through
Now I stand here and try to remember
The girl I discovered in my search for you

They say love doesn't ask for more than what it gets
So why did I always want a bigger piece of you?
In the crush of life I was sometimes lost in the crowd
Never sure if I ever came completely into view

But somehow I learned to be stronger
And somehow I'm certain you knew

CHORUS
But you left me in early December
You loved me but we both knew our time was through
Now I stand here and try to remember
The girl I discovered in my search for you

BRIDGE
You gave me the passion to find my way
You gave me the eyes to dream
If we squandered the time we had you've got to know
That what I searched to find in you I finally found in me

CHORUS
You left me in early December
You loved me but we both knew our time was through
Now I stand here and surely remember
The girl I discovered in my search for you
My search for you
My search for you

Originally recorded for my CD, Somewhere On the Way, *"My Search For You," was written for my father who died on an early morning in early December. It also became the theme song for "Tessa Curzio," the protagonist of my first novel,* After the Sucker Punch, *and was also included as a link in that book.*

Lyrics by Lorraine Devon Wilke, Music by LDW & Rick M. Hirsch
Photo courtesy of family archives.

To enjoy a listen, input the following link:

https://soundcloud.com/lorraine-devon-wilke/my-search-for-you

RACIE WALKER WAS A CHILD OF GOD

a mostly true story

RACIE WALKER WAS a Child of God. Or so her mother told her.

This numinous assignation, stated always in title form, was in direct correlation to Racie's role as a blessed and unexpected "late life baby," a second child whose arrival, years after her parents surrendered all hope of continued procreation, deemed her special.

Though her anointed name, Grace Mary Theresa Bernadette Walker, included enough saints to cement her vaunted status, it was her brother, four years her senior and struggling with the hard "G," who reduced that beatified moniker to the more secular "Racie." It stuck, despite admonitions to "use your sister's baptized name." Projected concerns about a nickname that might prove suggestive during the teen years held little sway over a guileless four-year-old.

As it was, the name didn't matter. Racie Walker *was* a Child of God as far as all were concerned.

The appellation wasn't explicitly known outside her immediate family, but she wore it like a talisman. At the small Catholic school that had been her scholastic home since first grade, a place of warm, childhood community, she was considered exemplary: her academics were solid, she made good friends and was routinely acknowledged for her respectful demeanor toward the priests and nuns of the parish. She was, by every known metric, a good girl.

But, as life is wont to do, change—unpredictable, unforeseeable change—came along. And somewhere within that maelstrom, Racie Walker was confronted by demands implicit to her title.

It started with shifting tenures at the school. Late that summer, a new teacher came to town who was assigned to Racie's upcoming 5th grade class. Sister Hildegard wasn't seven feet tall, but she might as well have been. She also wasn't "100-years-old," as some were convinced, but the drooping lines of her post-Bell's Palsy face, with its peculiar one-sided frown, carved a visage so fierce the children were both repelled and perversely fascinated. With the addition of a pronounced limp with its attendant clacking cane, and a clipped German accent that turned every statement into a bark, she loomed large and intimidating.

Racie was initially prepared to "rise above," as her mother suggested upon learning of her daughter's disdain for the new teacher, but, despite good intentions and worthy efforts, new information intervened. It would make that adjustment impossible.

Sister Hildegard had a "hitting stick," the term this Bride of Christ gave the weapon most often held in her gnarled hands. With a crucifix swaying on her chest as she waved said cudgel in the air, the juxtaposition was jarring.

Two-by-thirty-six inches, a good half-inch thick, this piece of varnished blonde wood was, as their wimpled tormentor announced weeks into the first semester, "incentive to stay on the right and tight path." It wasn't clear what, exactly, that meant—surely, she wouldn't inflict *actual* corporal punishment on her tender charges—but as she stood at the front of the room, thwacking her palm to punctuate the pronouncement, the idea that infractions would be met with muscle seemed very real.

Then they were.

Only one week later, a boy's knees were thumped after he threw an eraser in a moment of ill-timed jocularity. Another was smacked across the wrists when he snickered during morning rosary. By the week before Thanksgiving, a group of "hooligans," as they were deemed, had flouted the spitball rule one time too many and all the boys in class, involvement notwithstanding, were marched, gauntlet style, across the back of the room. As each passed their stick-wielding teacher, punishment was meted with fervor.

The first was a hard crack across the shoulders, loud and surely painful, but the leader of the gang "took it like a man"—as he later boasted—wincing without a word. The next blow elicited a yelp from a less hearty perpetrator. But the whack that caught the elbow of a smaller boy, who'd had no participation in the crime, came with a tearful whimper that grabbed Racie's gut.

Something about Sister Hildegard's bullying violence, that boy's muted vulnerability, as well as the fact that he'd been unfairly swept up in the dragnet, triggered a rage in Racie that she'd never felt before. So unfamiliar was that surge of homicidal adrenaline she almost burst into tears. Instead, she made a fierce determination, right then and there, that her status as a Child of God was of no use if it didn't enfranchise righteous response. Something had to be done.

This was the era of the Cold War, with its gray paranoia, doomsday zeitgeist, and legends of wild international spies, so it followed that espionage was inspired by the nun's brutality. Racie recruited three of her closest classmates, Pamela, Nettie, and Brian, instructing them to meet her in the church basement after school to discuss strategy. With the precision of a general, she led the high-pitched but largely amenable brainstorming session to its inexorable conclusion.

They were going to heist the stick.

Putting aside communal terror of their teacher, and with the grit and gravitas of resolute spies, they fine-tuned specifics to cover every detail: Nettie and Brian would be strategically placed lookouts; Pamela would be at the classroom door in the event of intervention; Racie would grab the stick from Sister Hildegard's desk drawer and transport it to the bridge above Nippersink Creek, the bucolic waterway they crossed to and from school. There, the stick would be dropped into rushing waters to be swept away forever.

It was a good plan; of that they were certain. They set the schedule, synchronized their timing, and after a makeshift prayer designed to ward off danger, they agreed to "act normal and keep it to ourselves," as Racie instructed.

Mission launch was to be the following Wednesday. That choice was based on Sister Hildegard's church visitation routine. She always stayed longer on Wednesdays when German prayers were included in afternoon services.

Upon the day's arrival, the air blew brisk, and sunlight bounced capriciously between darkening clouds. With after-school activities in full swing and the classroom empty, all parties took their positions. Racie felt queasy, aware that earlier bravado had lessened in the face of actuality, but before her fear could metastasize, she reminded herself that, as a Child of God, she had a holy obligation; this was her challenge to embrace.

She sat at her desk waiting stoically for the signal to commence. When reports of "enemy clear!" came down the line, Pamela's eyes flared, and she gave Racie the nod.

With *The Man from U.N.C.L.E.* theme pulsing through her head, Racie ran to Sister Hildegard's desk where she fumbled with the top drawer, relieved when it finally popped open. There it was. Tucked under a stack of lined penmanship paper, it appeared, somehow, less malevolent lying flat in the drawer than when dangling from Sister Hildegard's bony hands, but "never mind!" she quickly admonished herself, extracting the dreaded item. It was then that a terrible truth became clear: it was too long to fit inside her school bag. No matter which way she turned it, no matter how hard she tried to snap the clasp shut, one end stuck out.

She shot Pamela a look of panic. Thoughts of aborting flew silently between them, but both realized they were in too deep; the mission had to be played out. Racie shook off her trepidation and rammed the stick down as far as it could go, holding the bag shut with her sweaty fingers.

Nettie suddenly burst in with an update: for unknown reasons, Sister Hildegard had left church early and was now making her way to the school and "moving fast!" Racie snapped out of the fog of war, grabbed her remaining courage and the too-small bag, and with Pamela and Nettie as able escorts, rushed stealthily down the hall. Through the adjacent windows they could see the nun plowing across the playground, habit flapping like a demented bird as they made their hasty exodus in the opposite direction. The team couldn't help but feel a rush of triumph when they shot through the double doors leading outside and raced past the convent to the creek.

By now Brian had joined them, and as the four stood trembling at the bridge, they recognized the enormity of the moment. Mission accomplished. They'd done it. They were true liberators. They hooted and hugged as Racie pulled the stick from her bag and, with ceremonious flair, flung it high over the railing. They watched as it arched in dramatic descent, hazy sunlight catching it for one transcendent moment before it plopped gracefully … onto a pile of flotsam. Stuck. In full view. From the bridge. Near the convent. Where the nuns often walked.

They looked at each other in horror. Brian offered to climb down and attempt a remedy, but though the creek was a frequent playground at its more meandering bends, breaching the bridge at this particular high-water spot was strictly forbidden. Unwilling to add another layer of anarchy to the mission, or risk the life of her cohort, Racie asserted that the stick would likely be washed away during the night. With that tepid assurance, the team raced off in their respective directions.

That night a freeze moved in. Instead of being washed away, the stick froze in clear view: blonde, brazen, and easily detectable.

Racie and Pamela, crossing the bridge on their way to school that morning, peered down at this misfortune, stunned. They tried throwing rocks to break up the surrounding ice, but both were such miserable shots they never even got close. Ultimately, they had no choice but to leave it to the fates, to God, to whoever oversaw such noble escapades, heading to school far less ebullient than they'd been the day before.

Slipping into the classroom with hearts pounding, the girls collapsed into their desk chairs, assiduously avoiding eye contact with their collaborators. But the buzz swirling around them was palpable. Though they hadn't talked openly of their covert operation, somehow word got out—as things do in a small school—and a tingle of anticipation percolated.

Then she walked in. Sister Hildegard. A behemoth wrapped in black and white. With her limp seemingly more pronounced, her cane clacking louder than usual; her face twisted in a savage grimace, she was every kind of terrifying.

Nettie briefly gasped, but Pamela shot her a look so formidable that an immediate adjustment was made. The nun lumbered to her desk without a glance toward the unusually quiet assembly. She made a scene of dramatically opening her drawer and, with feigned surprise, looked up.

"And vhat's zis? It looks like someone has not only trespassed on my property but has stolen somezing of mine." The tone was chilling.

She came from behind her desk to pace the aisles like a prison warden, hands clasped behind as if useless now without her weapon. She stopped beside each student, boring into their face with x-ray eyes, attempting to gauge guilt or innocence.

Brian smiled like a goon, but that was his typical countenance, leaving nothing to trigger suspicion. Nettie ultimately found a placid expression to hold onto, one that—mixed with her reputation as a compliant sort—pulled her immediately off the hook. Pamela, taller and more mature than the rest of the girls, held Sister Hildegard's gaze with a certain defiance. Racie wasn't sure of the wisdom of that tact, but Pamela possessed an aura of impunity, based, in no small part, on the fact that her father had built much of the town. She, too, passed muster.

Racie's turn. She could feel the nun's slow approach from behind, her tentacles of suspicion sharp and unnerving. As Hildegard made her way to the side of her desk, she abruptly bent down; her ferocity shooting through Racie like a laser. There was a tremor of panic, but once that initial bolt passed, Racie realized her teacher's implied threat served only to bolster her fortitude. She held. Nothing escaped. Her face was inscrutable.

After a beat of silence, Sister Hildegard straightened up as if rebuffed. She clumped slowly to the front of the room, growling an edict behind her: "I *vill* find out who took my stick, and they *vill* be punished. And if anyone knows who that person is and doesn't speak up, they too vill be punished. MARK MY WORDS, CHILDREN!" She roared the admonition like a beast, leaving her audience deathly silent.

With her back to the room, the team glanced around with the tension of uncertainty. Would anyone crumble? Would anyone break? Would the fear of threatened assault push anyone toward capitulation?

Then, in a thrilling moment of solidarity, the boy whose elbow had been bruised days earlier silently raised his fist with a smile in Racie's direction. Before Sister Hildegard could turn around, that tacit message of support and gratitude pinballed around the room, and the team knew they were not only safe, they were heroes.

Later that day the sun came out, and when Racie and Pamela crossed the bridge home, they saw that the Nippersink had acquiesced to their adventure. The rushing waters had finally broken through the ice, sweeping all evidence of their caper past the convent toward waters unknown.

Just as Racie suspected it would.

She was, after all, a Child of God.

The End

There are people who know this story is essentially true, people for whom this caper was a seminal moment of grade school heroism. Some of the names have been changed to protect the guilty and brave. You know who you are. ☺

Photo courtesy of family archives.

THE SAME SWEET LULLABY

song for a child and mother

This was a house that was perfect and still but so empty
A world designed to keep out distractions love would let in
Driven by dreams that eluded but never stopped tempting
I found myself all alone waiting for life to begin

My mama said, "Ambition will not heal your heart"
My mama cried when I cried all alone
And she sang...

CHORUS
The same sweet lullaby I sing for you
The same sweet lullaby I sing for you
The same sweet lullaby I sing for you, for you

Then came love with a truth and a magic that led to you
I held you close and at once felt passion so fierce and so tender
How does a child have the power to alter our point of view?
The power to help us forget, to make us remember...

How my mama tried, she never set the world on fire
But she was there to keep us through the night
As she sang...

CHORUS
The same sweet lullaby I sing for you
The same sweet lullaby I sing for you
The same sweet lullaby I sing for you, for you

BRIDGE
Are we remembered for love or is it accomplishment?
Are we defined by the lessons we teach or we learn?
I'm bound to you with love so profound to be heaven-sent
My path and purpose defined by where you're concerned

My mama said, "Seek your dream, but walk now with your child"
"This mother's love will guide you on your way"
And she sang...

CHORUS
The same sweet lullaby I sing for you
The same sweet lullaby I sing for you
The same sweet lullaby I sing for you, for you

These lyrics, which I wrote to honor both my son and my mother, were composed for song that has never been properly recorded, but still I wanted to include them here. The melody, inspired by a musical track written by a frequent songwriting partner of mine, David Resnik, remains sweetly in my head. Someday I will record this lullaby . . . it's special to me and quite pretty.

Photo courtesy of family archives.

AGING WHILE WOMAN . . . HOW DARE WE?

an essay

WE LOVE THEM. We hate them. We honor them. We assault them. We stare at them. We look away. They please us. They make us hate who we are. Especially, oh, *especially* as we get older.

Faces. Women's faces.

They are the repository of everything we think, feel, know, or fear about who we are as physical embodiments. One need only spend a little time on Instagram or Tik Tok to see the staggering obsession that women—of all ages—have with their faces. Bodies, too, yes, of course, but for the purposes of this piece, and given how unavoidably visible faces are, let's keep the focus there. And why not? Isn't just about everything we see around us focused on *faces*?

I recently saw a photo of a very famous pop star (who shall remain nameless because this is not about specifically shaming anyone), and I only knew it was her because the caption said it was. Had it not, I might have guessed anyway but with significant dollops of incredulity. Because this particular pop star looked so completely alien to her former self that there was little resemblance to the "sassy chick" she'd been in the olden days of our mutual youth. And not because she'd gotten older, but because at some point *while* getting older she'd completely re-manufactured her face.

Which is sad. Because I liked her face. Now I couldn't find it.

Let's assume her cosmetic transformation was by choice—it's doubtful anyone could get this particular woman to do *anything* she didn't want to do. But let's also assume the choice was likely pressured by the fact that she's in an industry where youth and beauty are vaunted above all else, *all else*, and her having the audacity to do that unthinkable thing—aging while woman—would surely have made the world stop spinning and fans fall to their knees in wailing protest had she not put herself through the plastic factory of reconfiguration.

Which is also sad.

I'm not picking on this particular woman. I could just as easily have seen a photo of any one of the preternaturally glacial mugs of a variety A-list actresses, singers, influencers, etc., and felt the same urge to scream, "We *are* allowed to grow old, dammit!"

Except … we're not. Not really.

I read an *InStyle* article a while back in which Sarah Jessica Parker, rightfully defiant about the sexist, ageist "chatter" of fans disturbed by her visible aging, brilliantly remarked, *"I know what I look like. I have no choice. What am I going to do about it? Stop aging? Disappear?"*

Given the ageist bent of the American zeitgeist, it's likely a good number of people would have answered, "Yes. That's exactly what you should do. Disappear."

But they're wrong and she's right.

Her defiance, her willingness to continue putting that lovely, aging face forward to continue doing her excellent work is applause-worthy. And let's think about *that* for a moment: why should it take courage to put one's aging face forward? That it actually *does* is quite the commentary on how women are viewed in our current culture.

I love Sarah's aging face. I *understand* her aging face. Because mine is aging too. As is yours. We're all aging, every day, every one of us, whether that cherry-cheeked three-year-old or the spry twenty-something over there smirking while getting a "glow up." We're all in this together, just at different points of the trajectory, and with different philosophies about how to traverse it.

Sadly, there *is* another response to Sarah's question, one that's being articulated by many, many women who don't have her (or Helen Mirren's, or Jamie Lee Curtis's, or Linda Hamilton's, or Emma Thompson's) confidence to boldly embrace their age without interference. For them, Sarah's question, "What am I going to do about it?" would be answered with: "You're going to get thee to a cosmetic surgeon tout suite, and do any and everything possible, imaginable, available, to remove all evidence of your natural age, cuz, sister, we will *not* be defined by our lines, wrinkles, droops, sags, and soft bits!"

No, we are to be defined, apparently, by our willingness to conjure up youth at any cost.

I'm convinced it's a form of Stockholm Syndrome: We're held painfully captive by impossibly high and unnatural standards of beauty, then feel compelled, driven, almost mandated, to capitulate to those standards, putting ourselves under the knife and needle while smiling, "It's my choice" or "I'm doing it for *me*," and, okay, I get it, but damn . . . what a price to pay! *(Forgive the run-on sentence ...)*

And really, who says we all have to be *youthfully* beautiful? Why is that such a desperately sought goal? Can't it be enough to be "olderly" beautiful? Pleasant looking? Cute? Moderately attractive? Nice looking? Healthy? Vibrant?

Nah. "Youthfully beautiful" is the gold standard of physical existence. *Especially* as we get older ... because if you're considered *youthfully* beautiful, or at least some harmonic of "attractive for your age," there's forgiveness to be had for the audacity of growing older.

I get the pressure. I do. I have a mirror. I see things happening with my face that I don't love and wouldn't mind doing something about. I haven't. I won't. At least not the hardcore cut & paste stuff. Because beyond my basic squeamishness, I truly believe there's a point to be made about graceful aging, and it ain't about *erasing* it. It's *declaring* it. Wearing it. Proudly. With verve. With vitality. With conviction that aging beauty is still beauty, valid beauty, *enough* beauty, despite the fact that our culture has decided the beauty of youth is the *only* beauty worth keeping.

Which seems terrifically unfair given how many years (if we're lucky) we all live as "older people" with older faces. Our culture needs to change that narrative, but I don't see it happening. Just take the issue of subliminal media gaslighting:

Is it just me, or do those articles that preeningly headline, "(Famous person) just turned 55 and can you believe how stunningly gorgeous she looks??" drive you insane too? I read those and want to scream: "Sure, she looks stunningly gorgeous and so very much younger than what's considered normal for fifty-five years *because she's spent a fucking fortune remaking her face! Please don't pretend that's a natural visage, or that her perfected beauty should set the standard for everyday women or any damn one else living life outside the bubble of surgical compliance."* (I'm not called a "loudmouth" for nothing ...)

Truth is, most people can't afford it, or wouldn't put themselves at risk, or prioritize their "well-being dollars" on other less invasive methods of self-improvement, and therefore, don't, perhaps, look as "stunningly gorgeous" at fifty-five, sixty-two, or seventy-three as that celebrity/influencer/media personality. So please stop trying to convince us, dear media, that *they're* the norm and we're just ... *old.* It's a disservice and a lie. One that does real damage to women already struggling in a culture that now wants us to regress back to some version of "stay-at-home, baby-producing, husband-deferring trad wives and mothers."

I observe women in my own life, some close, some in my periphery, who've obviously availed themselves of surgical intervention (i.e., any woman over fifty with nary a line in her forehead is a dead giveaway), and, frankly, feel a mix of envy, curiosity, and sadness. Envy, because who doesn't want to be or look, as both Rod Stewart and Bob Dylan opined, forever young? (I do miss my formerly razor-sharp jawline, and the "eleven" between my brows is damn near a trench.) Curiosity, as I ponder how they navigated the cost, the risk, the potential damage of such intervention. And sadness, because it hurts my heart to think that the only way women can feel "empowered" (as someone I know put it), or "more me" (as another did), is to remove any vestige of their longevity, their having lived life, of their *being their age.*

Though, frankly, it's not just older women succumbing to this tortuous, expensive, sometimes self-mutilating response to aging. I'm seeing younger and younger women—particularly in the media industries, though certainly not exclusively—jump on that train as soon as a line shows up on their face, leading to a strange demographic of attractive young women who start early to resemble large, lovely, plastic dolls. *And each other.* The particular uniformity of visage that's evolved (devolved?) out of this trend, a very distinct look that's widely replicated, is puzzling. I don't understand why homogenized "beauty" is considered a good thing. I always felt uniqueness and individuality were more desirable traits, but those ubiquitous swollen lips, inflated apple cheeks, preternaturally taut jawlines, and foreheads tight as a drum are everywhere. It would seem uniformity and obvious intervention *are* considered better than *old*.

"What about men?" one twitchy gal feeling defensive on the topic queried me. "They're doing a lot of this stuff too, but I don't see you talking about them."

Yes. Yes, they are. I see it. I notice it. But still, even now, and regardless of how many men feel the pull of vanity enough to avail themselves of knives, needles, lasers, fillers, and supplements, I don't think anyone could debate that women are allowed far less latitude in terms of aging than men. Men have always been allowed to grow older with grace, with their jowls, graying hair, and "dad bods" considered lovable or distinguished, rather than "eww-inspiring."

I've taken to watching international television these days not just because their series tend to be quite good, but because I relish the opportunity to view men and women of certain ages who actually *look* those ages. That's a revelation, really, considering that most FBI agents, doctors, cops, teachers, nurses, or firefighters on American TV tend to look like models. I rarely experience that standard of perfection in real-life with such people, though given my (thankful) dearth of interaction with police or FBI, perhaps they've prettied up in ways I'm not aware of.

As for that aforementioned "aging" three-year-old: the difference between her and your sixty-something cousin Donna is that unlike the toddler, Donna is considered on the downslope of life and, therefore, reminds us of death. We don't like death, we don't like being reminded of death, so we don't like Donna. And even if we can put aside death as a trigger, we also don't like Donna because she's not as sexually appealing as Americans like their women, and once that happens, she's of no particular value. Kind of like Tudor wives who lost favor and therefore heads. We don't behead our women for aging; we just shame them into surgery.

We need to stop that. We need to evolve as a society past this sexist, ageist, self-flagellating attitude. Because it's only perception, not reality. Once it's been decided (as it has) that the only face of merit is a young one, we've demonized and made terrifying one of the most inevitable, unavoidable, and universally shared experiences of human life: aging.

Certainly we women have it within us to reject that script.

Because as one very evolved woman so beautifully put it to me: *"I embrace aging, as I've known a few people who would have loved the chance to get wrinkles or a softer jawline but didn't get enough time to. People need to recognize the privilege of aging rather than vilifying it."*

I couldn't have said it better myself.

Photo by Luis Machado

SHE TUMBLED DOWN

a short story

THE GRIT OF sand was sharp; the sense of surreal so strong there was no way to process the event unfolding. She felt speed and motion, the scraping of flesh as impact propelled her across the gravel. She'd often wondered how death would feel, what you'd think as it came upon you, *if* you'd think, but this moment unfolded in abrupt, poorly-edited jump cuts that left crucial details confused, hurling her blindly towards inevitable conclusion. No thoughts emerged … she just tumbled down until all motion stopped and everything went black.

Behind the shattered windshield he shook so hard he could barely breathe.

∞∞∞

Lainey Pastouras talked about parties and blind dates with a vigor that implied both were essential to the day, but Charlotte Frame, the reluctant birthday girl, had quite a different view.

"I want nothing more than Marjolaine cake, good champagne, and the joy of platonic friends."

"And I want to be instrumental in making you a little happier than you are now," Lainey persisted.

"I'm plenty happy. Marjolaine would be the tipping point."

"You're past due for a personal evolution, Charlotte. You've been lonely too long, you'll be forty-six on Friday, and it's time for love to round the sharper corners of your life."

Charlotte liked her sharper corners.

But she was also aware that embracing any element of the dating process would go a long way toward getting her circle of friends, particularly Lainey, off her lonely back. This had always been more easily pondered than done, however. Despite sincere appreciation for the rituals of romance, it remained true for Charlotte that finding men of merit was not easy in the 21st century. That it hadn't been much easier in the 20th century, when she was young and men of merit (or otherwise) were exponentially more receptive, was irrelevant to the conversation.

So in a moment of birthday vulnerability she relented, allowing her best friend to sell her on the idea of inviting someone she'd never met to a party she didn't want, with assurances that this invitee was a man of honor, financial solvency, and a "great ass." As much as Charlotte admired all three, she was generally against these sorts of amatory arrangements, convinced they were too forced and artificial to ever end well, but it *was* her birthday. And for some reason she felt anticipatory and so ripe for change that Lainey, with admirable statistics in finding good men in a haystack, seemed the perfect arbiter of that change.

The party was planned, Marjolaine cake was ordered, Hugh Raymond was invited and, to Charlotte's blushing surprise, he accepted.

Happy birthday, dear Charlotte, happy birthday to you.

∞∞∞

The leather seats of his car had a smell he'd always liked, a scent of luxury and impeccable taste. It was an expensive car and there'd been arguments about even considering the purchase so soon after they moved to the expensive house. But to him it signaled success and he told her as much. It would be good for "the brand," he insisted when she made comment about him showing off and "reaching beyond our means." Though she ultimately acquiesced, she never particularly liked the car . . . or the smell of those seats, which, she said, made her feel like she was riding around in a hide factory. He told her to get used to it; he'd never have a lesser car, he proclaimed.

Now, in this swirling moment of dust and panicked breath, those luxurious seats were sprinkled with glass shards and gravel bits and gave off an odor that struck him as gamey. Strange, really, how pungent it was. He'd never noticed that before and had the illogical thought that he'd have to mention it to his wife.

ꝏꝏꝏ

Charlotte hadn't had sex since the last half of the second year of her marriage, which was two years before her divorce, which was now four years ago. This was enough sexual downtime that the idea of letting a man she barely knew not only into her home, but her bed and her body was unfathomable at evening's commencement. By dessert the heat between her and her blind date was so palpable others circling the table graciously peeled off to the bar, where Lainey cast frequent glances back to revel in her success.

And success it was. Charlotte appeared to have lost all remnants of her characteristic wariness, embodying a version of herself no one could have pictured and she only imagined in late-night fantasies: hot, beautiful, and sexually rapacious. This translated, for the moment, into comically discreet but undeniably public displays of affection. Which, it seemed to her in the heat of the moment, were patently unavoidable.

Between breaths, she noticed Hugh wasn't drinking, which intrigued her. She'd had a couple, leaving her loose and receptive, but even so, she was typically more restrained. Retrospect later clarified that Hugh had simply melted her core.

Attractive as advertised, funny, articulate and just heedful enough to hold her attention, he exceeded every criterion in ways that both surprised and delighted her. He was a successful pediatrician, the father of two functional young men, divorced for two years, and clearly primed for his next chapter, given the lack of ambiguity in his flirtations.

The most immediate next chapter led to her home and the cocoon of her long-neglected bed, where everything changed amidst tenderness and hard passion. It was one of those nights when the ephemera of life shifts. The walls open, the ceiling rises, the air sweetens; even the hope of a better world is suddenly imaginable.

Love and sex may not possess such powers in reality, but on this night, in this bed, with this man, they were a force for good. Charlotte's good, in particular. Hugh was the healer of heart, and by virtue of his touch she became a new woman.

It was an excellent birthday.

∞∞∞

The whisper of branches tapping as the ocean breeze cleared fireworks from the post-midnight sky was the most salient sound that remained. In some distant place the laughter of New Year's Eve revelers still tinkled from time to time and the occasional car whizzed by on the adjacent street, but here the night was over. The revelry done.

There was no prolonged moment of disorientation or pain, no sliver of consciousness to clarify the unfathomable; no respite from the stunning fact of what had just happened. She lay tucked under a smattering of fallen leaves, half hidden and bent in ways bodies do not go; her face white and streaked with blood, her eyes lost in a glaze of shock. Hanging at the precipice with no awareness of the imminent fall.

And though alive as he'd been before colliding with a woman in a crosswalk, he knew his own life was now a thing of shifts and changes. Awash in booze and late-night weariness, he'd simply not seen her. In the same split-second she experienced, he could only watch as her body smashed into the windshield with a fearsome thud, then flew across the gravel and down the embankment.

The stillness that followed that unimaginable moment was eerie; horrible, jagged-breath silence as sweat poured down his cheeks. The redolence of leather he'd noticed in the moments before seemed to have ratcheted up to the point that he thought he would vomit, so he sat motionless long enough to quell the nausea and formulate a cogent plan.

He peered through the broken glass. There was nothing to see.

The night was dark, no cars approached; no one appeared. He leaned forward; was she lying there? Right there in front of his car? There was no movement he could detect, but dizziness hampered his view. More pertinently, he was profoundly inebriated, a state that left all logic and compassion elsewhere. His mind darted amongst various scenarios, each one more inconceivable than the next, until he ultimately rejected all but one.

He pushed aside the airbag, brushed the glass off the seats, restarted his engine, and tore away in a roar of gravel.

To crawl deeper into what was now an irrevocable event would surely end his own life, and that paralyzing thought drove him much too far to turn back.

∞∞∞

They were weeks into it now, lost in the moist, creamy center of new love, so exquisite that reason slipped through the cracks. But Charlotte wanted no part of reason anyway. Like a child, a needy thing, she craved only him, warm and real in her bed, wanting nothing but to curl into his love and stay there forever. Gratefully, he opened his arms to welcome her, and she tumbled down.

They laughed at their own besottedness. Both had endured enough heartache to find their mutual enthusiasm refreshing. They held tight and moved fast, unwilling to waste a moment on caginess or calculation.

Lainey was initially thrilled with the rapid advancement of her matchmaking, but when Charlotte announced she was moving into Hugh's stunning waterfront home, a matter decided only the night before, her response was muted. "Wow. I'm slightly stunned. Or are you joking?"

Charlotte, high on the fog of love, was immediately annoyed. "No, I'm not joking and why would you be stunned? You brokered the damn deal. Aren't you the one who's been lecturing me on the virtues of love for years now? I thought you'd be thrilled."

"I *am* thrilled. Thrilled that you're happy, thrilled that things are going well; I'm just stunned that you're moving so fast. It's only been … what? Three weeks?"

"It's been over a month and why is that relevant?"

Lainey cocked her head. "Charlotte. I've known you for over ten years and you're not a silly woman. You know why that's relevant."

"Oh, I see. You don't believe in love at first sight. And we're too old for that sort of thing anyway, right?" Charlotte sounded like a petulant teenager.

"No, I *do* believe in love at first sight—though in most cases 'lust' is the more appropriate word." Lainey winked; Charlotte rolled her eyes. "But what's also true, and what we *are* too old for, is believing we don't need time, real time together, to know if 'first lust' translates into *real* love."

Charlotte sat down with a thud and little-disguised pique. "Buzzkill."

They both laughed, though briefly.

But as Lainey poured another cup of coffee, Charlotte persisted. "Seriously though, I get all that, really, I do, but why are you being hesitant? Is it *specific* hesitance? Like, there's something about Hugh I don't know?"

"I'm sure there are many things about Hugh you don't know; it's only been a month! You'll get there, girlfriend. If you move in, you'll likely get there sooner than expected." Lainey glanced over to her brooding friend. "Why, are *you* worried?"

"No, he's … incredible. He's everything I could ever want. Which is why I'm terrified. Is it possible he's too good to be true?"

"Probably." Lainey laughed. Charlotte's flush of anguish indicated a more sensitive tack was in order. "Look, Char, in all the years I've known him, most of which were spent discussing my children's fevers and when to give them what medicine, he was never anything but a stellar guy. He went through a rough divorce, that was dicey for a while, but as far as I know everything is civil now. His boys are both spectacular, he's considered one of the best pediatricians in the city, and he has a busy pro bono clinic, so yeah; he's a pretty great guy. Which, if you remember, is why I wanted to fix you up with him in the first place."

"Then why do you think I should wait?"

"Because I'm a realist. And I think time can be useful. Trust me, Char, I'm all for this, but moving in is a big step. I just want you to be sure."

Charlotte sat pondering for a moment then looked up. "I'm sure." Quiet, definitive . . . sure.

So Lainey squeezed Charlotte's hand, and they went on to discuss what should be done with Charlotte's condo, if the longer commute would be a problem, and what, if any, hesitation she had about the potential of moving toward something even more permanent (none so far). It was a good girlfriend conversation.

Charlotte moved in with Hugh the next weekend.

ꝏꝏꝏ

He drove all night, fast and towards Tucson. His college buddy lived alone and on the margins; he would know a good body man and would ask few questions.

He wasn't expected home—that was his ace. He and his wife had decided earlier he'd stay at a hotel as a precaution against New Year's Eve drivers (the irony did not escape him). If he could get the necessary business done in twenty-four hours, he had a shot at pulling this off.

He'd conjured up a feasible story while stopped along the way to wipe down the car. By the time he was in his friend's kitchen sipping coffee, braced against the effects of a fierce hangover and the burgeoning wash of doom, it was late morning with no time to waste.

"It was a chickenshit thing to do, I admit, but I was so fucking drunk I just took off. I couldn't even tell you exactly where I was when it happened."

"I'm surprised you were in Tucson and stayed at a hotel. You could've stayed here."

"Yeah, thanks . . . I got in right before the party—a business thing you would've hated, or I'd have called earlier. Anyway, after I smashed up the car I thought I'd head over; figured you could recommend somebody, and we'd catch up while it was getting fixed."

"So, you just hit another car while you were trying to park?"

This was the conversation he did not want to have. "Actually, I slammed into one of those pillars—you know, in those underground lots? Knocked a chunk of cement onto the car—"

"Jesus Christ!"

"It wasn't that big, but it sure did a number on the windshield."

And so the fiction went. They discussed the urgency of getting the car fixed quickly enough to keep his wife out of the loop; it was understood that a man with a drinking problem didn't need a wife alerted, if that could be avoided.

There was a guy working on the car by noon with promises he'd have it done by the next morning. The fee for the rush job was hefty but need discouraged haggling. Calls were made home about staying another night (blamed on a killer hangover), a minor argument was quelled, the car got fixed, and he was back to work by late afternoon the following day.

Life went on.

For him.

ꝏꝏꝏ

The morning of January 1st brought teams of police investigators who scoured the street side, particularly the gully where she'd been found. The gravel was sifted for any clue: pieces of broken headlight, paint chips, even a footprint that might hint at who had been there and who had done this. Detectives knocked on the doors of nearby residents, many still recovering from celebrations of the night before and all stunned to hear a woman had died in such close proximity and without their awareness.

But no one had seen or heard anything. Cameras captured nothing. No clues were found. No calls came in. It was as if the event occurred in a vacuum . . . a life ended without the slightest notice of the world around.

∞∞∞

Hugh was seeing clinic patients the day of her move-in, and after the workers she hired had finally left (there were issues with an unwieldy chair and a particularly narrow hallway), Charlotte took time to walk through this place she now called home. She'd already spent many a delightful day and night there in the weeks leading up to the move but viewing it as a resident offered new perspective.

It was simply a stunning place. So far beyond her rather industrial condo (now on the market) she could only think, "I live here now!" with an impossibly smug grin. The three-story Craftsman was surrounded by palm trees and gorgeous landscaping, burnished gold by sunlight reflecting up from the nearby beach. The setting made her feel as if she'd just booked an extended vacation, triggering a sense of giddy well-being that offset any (albeit slight) panic she felt about the move.

She went from room to room, paying close attention to his decorating choices and thinking about where her few pieces of art and furniture might go. When she got back to the living room, she opened a box of her framed photos and pulled a few out to place on the mantle along with his rather large collection. She decided they fit right in.

Charlotte stood back and made the general assessment that her new roommate was a man of unassailable taste who enjoyed surrounding himself with beautiful things and the reminders of family, friends, and love. Which made her realize she was completely happy to be there. Even more so when she wandered into the kitchen to find a French press ready to go and a plate of her favorite scones with the note, "Welcome home!"

ꝏꝏꝏ

In the weeks that passed, every streetlight pole near the crash site had been plastered with fliers about the hit-and-run. Her picture—beautiful, smiling, alive—was centered amongst words overflowing with rage and sorrow:

"A coward destroyed our family …"

"If you have any knowledge of the driver …."

"She was beloved by her family and friends …"

"Please help us find her killer …"

"Contact the police if you know anything …"

"There's a reward for any information leading to an arrest."

"We love you and miss you …."

"Who could do this and drive away?"

ꝏꝏꝏ

At first it was awkward. There was no getting around it. Rhythms would clash; habits would collide. They'd discovered earlier that both preferred to sleep on the right side of the bed, and neither was sure who should concede in this more permanent arrangement. When Hugh did, Charlotte felt guilty. He promised he was adaptable and was.

His sons came for dinner and that went surprisingly well. Both in their early twenties, they were young enough to remain charmingly attached to their father but with enough maturity to realize families can change and still be something good. She could tell they liked her and, though it was too soon for predictions, she hoped by Thanksgiving their house would be the destination of choice.

There were days when she missed her condo (now sold); the privacy, the aloneness, the sense of *hers*, but mostly she enjoyed the larger home with its gourmet appliances and high-end appointments. They'd moved her few pieces of furniture into select rooms, her pictures onto various walls, and he was generous enough to allow her Crate and Barrel to replace the Wedgewood he'd had for years. Hugh, in fact, seemed willing to accommodate anything. Which puzzled her.

"I'm just so happy you're here," he explained.

"Why?" she asked, authentically curious. She'd been alone for so long it was hard to imagine anyone being *that* happy she was anywhere.

"I feel like I've been looking for you my whole life and you're finally here. Furniture and dinner plates are easy; finding you was not. I've got my priorities straight." He smiled.

Then he pulled her down to the living room Persian and fucked her like a man in love, making clear his priorities in that department.

∞∞∞

There was nothing to assuage their piercing anguish, no news; no hope. The family asked all the right questions of whomever they could ask, they did all the right things that were asked of them; they answered every query, offered every piece of information, but still . . . nothing. Knowing that justice moved further away with each passing day was a tear of the soul that made healing impossible.

The police were compassionate with them and relentless in their pursuit, and the investigation continued unabated, but they were told, "only one out of five hit-and-run cases is ever solved." Given the dearth of witnesses or any useful evidence, their lead investigator grimly informed them that their case would likely be one of the four that wasn't.

Which they refused to accept. It simply couldn't be. They kept the street memorial fresh with fliers and plastic flowers; locals were repeatedly questioned by various members of the family; even social media was put to task in hopes of ferreting out the perpetrator or a witness who might have seen something or heard something.

But those early weeks of the new year rolled on and on to become the later weeks of the spring, then the summer, into the fall with nothing gained.

Except the shattering awareness that she was dead and whoever was responsible had vanished along with her.

∞∞∞

"He finally said he loved me."

Lainey looked at Charlotte with some surprise. "I should *hope* so . . . you moved in with the guy!"

"Don't be dense. I'm simply confirming, for your cynical edification, that it's not *just* lust, as you so crassly suggested. Whatever it might have been at first sight, it is now real, true, hardcore love."

Charlotte was beaming so ridiculously that Lainey spared her a snappy rejoinder; she just grinned and hugged her friend with real feeling. "Then I'm happy for you, Char."

But no one was happier than Charlotte. There was something about Hugh's love that was transcendent. It soothed her, gave her confidence; put solid ground beneath her feet. And she could bloom on solid ground.

She now understood what they meant by, "You just know."

She knew.

∞∞∞

It just took compartmentalizing. He was good at it. He'd done it in every relationship, all through school, as needed in his profession, even in finding the balance between family and solitude. Now he was learning to annul the fact that he was a murderer. A coward. A person who could end a life and walk away without a thought.

Except that wasn't true. He thought about it almost every minute of every day. When he touched his wife he thought about the startled face slamming into the windshield just inches from his own. When he spent time with his kids he thought about her family and the horror and grief they must be feeling. When he did his work he wondered if she did something important and meaningful in her life. When he scoured the papers and realized no one had seen him, he felt both relief and shame. When he drove past the corner and saw fliers on the streetlight poles he was ripped by guilt. And when he picked up one of those fliers and saw the pretty, smiling face of the young woman whose life he'd ended, he knew the only way he could survive this was to put it all—every detail, thought, and gut-ripping emotion—into a box somewhere deep in his psyche where no one could tread and scars could grow until nothing was left but the hump of forgotten, dismissed memory.

∞∞∞

Charlotte responded unabashedly and unequivocally. After ten months of passionate and ultimately compatible cohabitation, Hugh asked her to marry him, and she said, "Yes." She'd wondered if she would ever utter that word to that question again in her lifetime and it turned out she would. All it took, it seems, was Hugh.

They lay in bed that night, warm in the intimacy of their new decision, staring into each other's eyes as if life itself could be found there.

"You know I love you with everything in me," she whispered.

"I do know. And I love you the same."

She curled into his chest, tucking her head into the crook of his neck as if she couldn't get close enough. "You have all of me, Hugh. I'll hold nothing back, I promise you that. I want you to know everything about me and I want to know everything about you, our past, present, and future. Do you know what I mean?"

He was quiet for a moment, pulling her closer still, until he finally answered. "I do, sweetheart . . . I do."

They set the date. April. It would be a lovely spring wedding. Small, intimate, just a few friends . . . lovely.

∞∞∞

He convinced himself it was her, her dissatisfaction with their lives, her frustrations with her career, her sense of conflict between working and being a mother. It all added up to a wife who was angry and bitter and profoundly unloving. She accused him of being shut down, of being detached and cold. She said he was "different." He dismissed the notion, enumerating her many rejections, both physical and emotional, adding that she didn't make it easy to be close. They argued constantly, spent their free time apart and did little together as a family. Before long they were talking to lawyers and by the next New Year's Eve, they were divorced.

In some ways, it was easier. He no longer had her to consider. He no longer had her to hide from. He no longer had her there as a female to remind him of anything female. He was glad she was gone. He was sick of her anger and neediness. He had his own needs. None of this was easy. Even time with the children was hard.

Over the months the fliers had disappeared from the light poles, but the plastic flowers and sorrowful notes remained. His office was nearby, and he drove that way often, though never sure why. Was it picking the scab or just the most direct route?

There was something about those poignant, faded flowers that pricked an irrational bone of contention with him. At what point was it over? At what point do people move on? Yes, it was tragic, it was a horrible thing, but it was an *accident*. There was no malice. No intent. His coming forward now would change nothing. It wouldn't bring her back. There would be no closure in it. It would only ruin more lives: his, his children's, his family's. He was remorseful, surely, but *there was nothing he could do*. Those damn purple flowers were hyperbole at this point. He wanted to tear them down.

Once he moved to the other end of town he made a point of driving a different route.

∞∞∞

The holidays were over, and it was time to plan a wedding. It was to be very small, so no monumental tasks were required, but even the less monumental ones didn't appear to be happening organically. As weeks went by and logistics mounted, and despite Lainey's occasional contributions, Charlotte was beginning to feel abandoned to the project. Nothing had changed between them, at least nothing of note, but she'd expected Hugh's involvement and wasn't getting it . . . at least not so far.

She came home Friday night with a plan to discuss this abdication and hopefully spark new enthusiasm for moving things forward. She found him in the living room sipping bourbon, remarkable only in that he hadn't had a drink the entire time she'd known him. "I didn't realize you … drank." She hoped her voice sounded as light and unconcerned as intended.

"I like a taste now and then."

"I didn't know that. I thought you said you weren't a drinker."

"Charlotte, I don't think having a drink now and then makes me a *drinker*!"

"I'm not criticizing; I'm just surprised, that's all. It's not an issue, Hugh, believe me."

"It's not an issue for me either, sweetheart. I just felt like a drink tonight." He quickly deflected to other topics—wisely, topics related to the wedding—and she was relieved. At one point, apropos to nothing, he grabbed her and held her long enough that it almost began to feel awkward. She looked up quizzically, but he just said, "I love you so much." She smiled and told him she loved him too, and they went back to discussing the guest list and if it was necessary to provide dancing for so small a crowd. He promised he'd be better about contributing to the event's organization, and they went to bed enveloped in their familiar intimacy.

But later that night she awoke to find him gone from the room. The clock said 3:17 and his absence at that hour was notable. Some internal tremor started at that exact moment, a tick of … something. She didn't know what it was, didn't know if she was just being dramatic, but it was unmistakable: something had shifted in the atmosphere. She climbed out of bed and tiptoed downstairs.

No lights, no sound, but the moonlight flooding through the picture window caught him in the leather chair by the fireplace. His head was bowed in his hands. He appeared to be sleeping or crying and the bottle of bourbon was now empty. The knot in her stomach grew exponentially as she approached. He looked up, his face a mask of inexplicable torment and, without a word, she knew her ticking dread was about to be realized.

∞∞∞

For three years they'd received anonymous donations at the preschool founded in her name. She'd been working toward an early childhood development degree before she died, and the family started the school to both honor her memory and offer an active channel for their grief. Donations were plentiful, particularly in the first year, but every month since the hit-and-run an envelope arrived with no return address, postmarked from various locations around the city, and always with a significant cash donation. The first one came with a simple note: "Because your daughter deserved better." Given the sentiment, they accepted it as a generous contribution from someone for whom their tragedy resonated. They were deeply grateful.

∞∞∞

There was no way to prepare for this. No way to adjust, brace, find a position that allowed plot points to unfold without impact. Charlotte sat frozen in the chair and listened to this unrecognizable man tell her something she couldn't possibly have conjured up in any moment of perverse imagination.

He started by echoing that he wanted her to know everything about him, too. She was pure and honest, and he'd already ruined one marriage, he said, he didn't want to ruin another. And so the box he'd packed away those three long years ago, the one filled with that horrible act and its many tentacles of guilt and shame, was dragged from its hiding place so he could "come clean and be the man you believe me to be." He said he owed her that.

He told her everything: the night, the drinking; the moment. It was a moment, he insisted, "anyone could have had"; a moment of sloppy driving, impaired reflexes, a wrong place/wrong time scenario that turned a random act into catastrophe.

She sat silently as he relayed his horror, his panic; his regret. He described the disorientation and drunkenness that not only twisted his judgment but impelled his urge to flee. He kept talking, kept adding details, hoping to fill the gaps, give her time to process, allow some element of redemption to emerge from this horrible tale. He talked without interruption until she finally stopped him.

"You just left her? You didn't get out to see if she was alive?" Her affect was flat, devoid of feeling. An investigator just looking for the facts.

"I thought about it and—"

"But you didn't go check?"

"No," he said without emotion.

Her body seemed to collapse inward, as if the truth of that statement was a gut-punch. She looked at him with anguish and suddenly howled, "*How could you not go back*? How could you not try to save her? *HOW*?"

Hugh felt a dark, familiar wave of nausea as he stumbled to reply. "I . . . I understand why you'd ask that, Charlotte, of course I do, but I can't explain it any better than I have. It was an unconscionable thing to do; I agree. I should have stayed. I should have gotten out of the car and checked on her, dialed 911, yes. I'm not making excuses, but I was incredibly drunk, not thinking clearly, and I panicked. Clearly I was in shock; I *wasn't* thinking, and by the time I was, I was hundreds of miles away."

Charlotte's eyes closed for a moment, then she lurched forward and vomited on the carpet as if there was simply no way to stop herself from doing so. He didn't move. When she sat up, she wiped her mouth with her sleeve and looked at him with the deadness she felt. "I don't know who you are."

His face tightened as if somehow he'd expected a different response, expected her to understand at least some part of this, expected love to trump judgment. But all he could say was, "I don't know who I was then either. I'm not that person now."

"But you went on with your life, didn't you? Just pretended it never happened, as if she didn't matter."

His head bowed again. "No, Charlotte … it wasn't like that. I was—"

"*She was a person!* She had people who loved her! How could you not stand up and take responsibility for what you did? How does somebody do that? You're a *doctor,* for God's sake!!"

He stood now as if suffocating under the weight of her reaction and all the guilt, all the justifications and manipulations, he'd been balancing all these years and was balancing still. "That's right, Charlotte, I'm a doctor. So I took my shame and guilt and became the best damn doctor I could be. Why do you think I started the clinic? It was something good to offset what I'd done. I've sent money to them every month, to their school for her . . . it doesn't make up for anything, I know, but it was what I could do!"

She said nothing. He was pacing now, desperate to convince her.

"Don't you think I was sick about it? *Am* sick about it? Charlotte, my God, I've been torn up about this thing since it happened. I ended a woman's life, which basically ended my own. I lost my marriage; I almost lost my boys. For the first few months I could barely make it into the office and almost lost that. But time went on and at some point it felt too late. I kept thinking, what will that do anyway, if I come forward? It won't change anything; it'll just destroy another family. It'll destroy my practice and all the people who depend on me there. I'll end up in prison not doing a damn good thing for anybody, and when I considered all that, none of it made sense."

Her voice barely reached above a whisper: "It's not about making sense ..."

"Charlotte, I . . . I know it sounds callous; I do. If it were my daughter I'd want to kill the man who did what I did. They probably *do* want to kill me. But I honestly kept thinking the best thing I could do was just live the most productive life I possibly could. So I helped her family—and I will always help them. I help the people who need me; I even quit drinking—at least until tonight when I knew I was going to tell you. I consciously became the best possible man I could be, for her, for myself, for my kids . . . and now for you. Doesn't any of that make sense?"

She was done listening. Charlotte got up as if everything inside her hurt and walked slowly out of the living room and up the stairs without a word of response. She went to the guest bedroom, crawled into the right side of the bed, curled into a fetal position, and forced herself to sleep.

Hugh sat in his chair until the sun came up. Then he cleaned the carpet around her chair, took a shower, and went to the office. He had several sick kids to see, a couple of new-parent meetings, and a training session with a nurse practitioner. It would be a very full day.

ထထထ

Some of it *did* make sense.

Charlotte called in sick, unable to imagine discourse with anyone on this gut-wrenching day after, and she was now pacing the house, roiling through every thought that shoved forward until she came to the unfathomable conclusion that Hugh's resolution did make some kind of sense. *Some* sense.

By midday she was sobbing uncontrollably at the inevitable loss of everything she had known and was anticipating. How could this *not* signal the disassembling of their impending marriage, of her sense of security and happiness? Despite the rage she felt and the urge to banish him forever, she mourned him as well, already feeling the shift in his role as her protector, her lover and best friend. Who could he be to her now? What could he be? He was a stranger, completely and utterly unknown.

What she couldn't think about yet was the woman. Not yet. That would come and, when it did, she knew it would do something to her, to them, that was impossible to predict in this churning moment of agony. She would have to take this in stages.

When Hugh came home that night Charlotte told him, "It did make some kind of sense." She was pale and distant when she said it; he saw that and didn't push, didn't ask too much, but clearly he was relieved.

She had tried to picture the alternative, and it felt too drastic, too punitive. He wasn't a monster; he was a good man, a good doctor. He was essential to so many people. He was doing his best to make amends. It was an accident.

They went to bed together and he held her quietly. They fell asleep without a word.

∞∞∞

Two weeks went by, and they tiptoed around each other as if surrendering to the silence that had now descended. Certain interactions came with some semblance of normalcy, but even those were strained and difficult. He said he understood that it would take time, and she mumbled inane comments in agreement. They didn't make love. They didn't talk about the wedding. She didn't return Lainey's calls. Work was her only respite.

On Wednesday of the third week after, Charlotte knew it was time to start thinking about *her*. The woman. With dread and an overwhelming sense of obligation she began researching accidents that occurred in the area on New Year's Eve three years earlier. It wasn't hard to find.

Cecilia Azuela.

The photographs depicted a beautiful young brunette with

sparkling eyes and a big smile. Twenty-one-years-old, a college student and preschool teacher; living with her parents and engaged to a long-term boyfriend. There were many friends, given the number of emotional testimonials in various articles, and families whose children she had worked with during her summers, all of whom were devastated at the incalculable loss of this bright young woman. Clearly she'd been deeply loved.

The circumstances that led up to the event were so banal and commonplace they almost seemed to mock the gravity of what followed. There had been a minor fight with her boyfriend at a New Year's Eve party, just a normal, everyday fight that anyone could have had on any day. But on this day, on this evening of holiday celebration, Cecilia had just enough champagne to make the foolish decision to head out alone at 12:25 a.m. to walk it off—the fight *and* the champagne. According to witness statements, she told her boyfriend to give her some space, and she'd be back in a while. Evidence indicated she was in a crosswalk on a dark neighborhood street a few blocks from the party when she was hit. Her body was discovered about forty-five minutes later by her worried boyfriend and his sister.

The coroner said she succumbed to severe internal bleeding, likely within a half-hour of impact. When asked, he confirmed that she might have been saved had she received immediate medical attention. There were no witnesses, no clues, the driver left the scene, and no one came forward.

No one ever came forward.

∞∞∞

The house was chilled and oddly quiet when he opened the door. He walked in heavy from the exhaustion of the day and the weighty anticipation of continued strain between him and Charlotte. On the way home he tried to pull together some benign topics to talk about, things to connect them, to somehow redeem him in her eyes, at least enough to start the process of getting past this. They *had* to get past this, he thought, or they didn't have a chance. And he wanted them to have a chance. He wanted that more than anything in the world.

He put his keys down and took off his jacket before he noticed: her pictures were gone from the mantle. He looked around with a sense of panic then ran quickly up the stairs to the bedroom and, like a bad cinematic cliché, empty hangers swung in her closet. He was stunned.

And just beyond his shock was the illogic of betrayal. He'd finally told the truth, he thought; was there really no redemption in that? Was he impossible to forgive, even by the woman who loved him most?

He ran back downstairs hoping to find evidence that would clarify what was already clear. The note was propped on the dining room table, short and to the point. "I'm sorry. It stopped making sense."

Under the saltshaker was a printout of an article with Cecilia's smiling face. Circled in bright red was the line, "might have been saved had she received immediate medical attention."

With that, Fate flooded over him like a tsunami. He dropped to the chair, staggered by the implications of what would follow, as disoriented and fearful as he'd been that horrible night. This time there was nowhere to run; that, he knew.

∞∞∞

Charlotte lay curled in the bed of Lainey's upstairs guestroom. Promises had been made to ask no questions. It was clear there was nothing frivolous or temporary about this refuge. Lainey could see that and, with a best friend's compassion, retreated downstairs without a word. There would be time for those later.

Charlotte could feel nothing, nothing but the hard beating of her heart. It was as if the breadth and width of her emotion was a thing so immeasurable, so ungraspable, that she could not yet open it up. She needed it to stay whole and undissected, big enough to block any piece of him, any view of him; to keep him as far from her thoughts as possible. Resolutions were forming but not yet clear and she needed to make those without thought of him.

She did think about forgiveness. She'd always believed one should be willing and capable of forgiving, even the most heinous of deeds. Like this one. Maybe one day she would be able to do that: forgive him. But she couldn't live with him, she couldn't marry him, and she could never understand how he'd been able to live with himself and what he had done. To Cecilia Azuela. To beautiful, young, hopeful Cecilia Azuela.

Charlotte closed her eyes and held her phone close, wondering if she was waiting for his call, or waiting for the call she would make. All she could do right now was hold the phone.

∞∞∞

Hugh sat hunched over the table in his kitchen, waiting as well. No lights were on; a bottle of bourbon sat open and nearing empty. There was nothing to do but wait . . . in this big, beautiful house where he'd hoped to build a new life. Wait until he knew what he was waiting for. For her next move, for his own conscience, for whatever Fate would finally bring to his door. Try though he might to concoct a different ending to the story, there was none.

He knew his turn had come . . . his turn to tumble down.

The End

The percentage of pedestrian deaths caused by hit-and-runs is around 20-25%, incidents that make up approximately 10% of all vehicle accidents in the United States. Tragically, relatively few are solved, as low as 20% in some states.

This particular story was inspired by one such hit-and-run that occurred in my neighborhood, one that, to this day, has not been solved and likely never will be. The street memorial put up by the victim's grief-stricken friends and family remained for several years and is the poignant image I captured for the cover of this story. I often walked past that memorial and, each time I did, couldn't help but wonder, "What kind of person could do such a thing . . . hit someone then drive away?"

"She Tumbled Down" is my imagining of one painful answer to that question. It is not the story of the woman who died on the street corner I walked by so often, but it is written in her honor and that of other hit-and-run victims whose heartless deaths will never find justice.

Photo by LDW

WHAT BARRY WHITE TAUGHT ME ABOUT LOVE

an essay

WHEN I WAS a young girl, electric with sensuality and burgeoning curiosity about all things lust, passion, and love, a song came on the radio that seemed an anthem to all three. I was working my first waitress job at the time, an Irish restaurant that had a jukebox stocked with as wide a range of radio hits as you'd expect, and in the midst of milquetoasty selections like, "Dancing In the Moonlight," and "The Morning After," was Barry White's, "I'm Gonna Love You Just A Little More." Remember?

I can still hear the suspense of that undulating, unforgettable intro: the drums start it, then the keys set that iconic riff; Barry's sultry voice weaves in and out in that bedroom way he had, a rumbling baritone crooning about love and need and passion so strong it couldn't possibly ever end. Every bit of it flowed together to create a grooving, driving, layered anthem to immutable love, and I was smitten.

I would play that song over and over, all day and into the night shift, swooning around "section B" like a lovesick teenager to the point that the bartenders thought I was crazy and every drunk in the room wanted to dance with me. But this wasn't about hook-ups and flirtations; this was about LOVE in all caps, a love so true it was indestructible. That's what I wanted, what I longed for: to be in love with someone who'd love me back with the same fierce, indestructible passion. Melodramatic, perhaps, but I was mesmerized by poetry and R&B-flavored enchantment, and I now had my love theme.

But as time went on, music changed; Barry put out other songs I liked but none quite as well. I grew up, fell in and out of love more times than my mother appreciated, and learned that the kind of passion Barry rhapsodized about wasn't so easily found. I still believed in it, hadn't given up on it, but stopped holding every relationship to the standard of *no way out*. I always seemed to find plenty of ways out ... or they did.

Until I met him. The man I married, the man who told me by virtue of everything he was, everything he had, and everything he promised on our wedding day that he would, indeed, give it all, that indestructible *all.*

And in the ensuing decades he has ... every joyful moment, every event, triumph, and memorable experience you could imagine. But life being what it is—meaning, we weren't actually living in a love ballad—we also hit some walls that were so damn hard I thought our heads would crack. His almost did. And those were the moments when *no way out* felt more like a sentence than a promise. We ebbed and flowed, ran away and came back; sought and suffered and looked and learned in every way we knew how and, somehow, some way, against all odds, we ended up full circle, back where we started ... back home. Where we healed and evolved and let go and forgave until we knew, once again, that we were indestructible. A vow coming full circle.

I'm sure you realize there's a wink in how I'm framing this story, a clear understanding of my sweet, youthful naiveté in believing love could be defined by a ballad sung by Dr. Love. But still ... certain ideas nestle, sensations and feelings become part of one's cellular memory, and even seemingly trite words and melodies become connectors to grander ideals. And, to this day, whenever I hear, "I'm Gonna Love You Just A Little More," I'm back at that juke box, swaying to the beat, eyes closed and heart filled with longing, believing in life and passion and tender expressions of everything that makes love grand and true.

And every year on our anniversary I celebrate the man I married, the one who spoke his own tender expressions so long ago, and speaks them still, and I say, "Happy Anniversary, darling. Wherever we've been, wherever we're going, however old we get, I'm always going to love you a little more."

Photo courtesy of family archives.

I SURRENDER

song for a husband

We have all been taught that love's an elusive thing
Battle-worn, we fought when love was the offering
Here we are, you and me, with only our hopeful hearts
So afraid to believe but somehow the fire starts

CHORUS
So I surrender to you
Oh, I surrender to you

Can you really be the one I've been looking for?
A man in love with me who's asking for nothing more
Do I wish on a star or pray that it's all I dreamed?
But somewhere in your arms I found you held everything

CHORUS
So I surrender to you
Oh, I surrender to you
Baby, I surrender to you
Oh, I surrender to you

BRIDGE
Love only asks that we give ourselves
A precious price that we find so hard to pay
But I give you myself
I give you myself
Oh, I give you myself

CHORUS
Oh, I surrender to you
I give you myself, baby
I give you, I give you myself
Oh, I surrender to you
I surrender

"I Surrender" was written for two audiences, two purposes. Included in the soundtrack of the film, To Cross the Rubicon, *I performed it onscreen as part of my character's story line. It was, however, more personally penned for the man I married, a heartfelt acclamation of the joy I felt in finally finding him, the one I'd been looking for.*

Lyrics by Lorraine Devon Wilke, Music by LDW & David Resnik
Photo courtesy of family archives.

To enjoy a listen, input the following link:

https://soundcloud.com/lorraine-devon-wilke/i-surrender-written-by

THE PURSE AND THE PUSH

creative non-fiction

A FAMILIAR SCENT of bleached cotton. The crisp edge of an ironed pillowcase. Both frame my face as I burrow deep in the comfort of the staircase bedroom at my grandmother's house. Beyond the quaintness of her knick-knacks and the Greek fabrics draped across the furniture, this spot is cherished for its privacy and stillness, two elements missing in the chaos of my life. I gaze up at the tilted ceiling that runs beneath the stairs leading to the second floor, my first childhood home, and relish the sweetness of this sanctuary.

My grandmother's Chicago was a mecca to me, particularly as I grew older and better able to assess my own sensibilities. Outside the womb of her beloved home, the city's electrifying bustle was in sharp contrast to the plains and hills of the farm town we moved to when I was young enough to forget Chicago's urban appeal. But trips back always reminded me: it was the color and diversity of life swirling around my grandmother that stirred my restless imagination.

All of nineteen when she emigrated from Turkey in the early years of the twentieth century, my grandmother joined Chicago's burgeoning Greek community to marry an austere train conductor many years her senior, a kind but dour man who gave his wife a decent—if unromantic—life, along with a two-flat on Victoria Street and a pair of handsome sons. My father was the younger.

They were modest people who took their new citizenship seriously, so intent on assimilation they taught neither son the language of the "old country." But even without its words, Greek culture permeated every aspect of their lives. Friends and relatives of the immigrant community became the foundation of their social circle, every meal was comprised of cuisine from the homeland, and, while they eschewed membership in the Greek Orthodox Church, it was understood the boys would "marry Greek."

Neither did.

My uncle wed a waspy, redheaded divorcée we later deemed glamorous, while my father took his own cultural rebellion a step bolder. He fell in love with an Irish/German Catholic girl with crooked teeth, an infectious laugh, and devotion to a faith that demanded commensurate devotion from whomever she might wed. Since marriage was the plan, and his passion for her was profound, conversion was swift, thorough, and equally passionate: he became a true Vatican soldier.

While my grandparents could accommodate one son's disregard of ethnic expectation, the second son's embrace of a religion they found even more anathematic than Greek Orthodoxy proved a tipping point from which they could not quickly recover. They were notably absent from the wedding, though my mother assures me she and my father were unbowed.

Somehow a shaky truce was later achieved, leading to an invitation to move our family into the upstairs flat of the Victoria Street house. This was likely due to my grandmother's desire to be close to her growing covey of grandchildren, but given my parents' limited finances, undoubtedly it was in their best interest as well.

Family lore depicts this as a difficult period of clashing sensibilities: my mother, raw and emotional, my grandmother, judgmental and terse. Yet home movies archive "Mad Men" cocktail parties with my beautiful parents and their equally attractive friends; Greek gatherings of horos dancing and tables replete with Kourambiethes and Koulourakia (favorite Greek cookies), honey-soaked diples (fragile phyllo desserts), and steaming pots of dolmades (meat-and-rice-filled grape leaves). My two older sisters and I appear smiling and happy throughout, with smudged faces and perpetually dirty feet as we romped through grubby yards, and in and out of alleys and gangways.

But selective chronicling couldn't mask the strain. When my mother became pregnant with her fourth child, my first brother, there was no denying we'd outgrown the upstairs flat, convenient rationale for flight. My father's push for distance drove him north, to what was likely the smallest farm town in all of Illinois, nearly to the border of Wisconsin, where barren neighborhoods of muddy lots somehow inspired his first foray into home ownership. A model was chosen, the house was built, and at the tender age of three, I was trundled from my grandmother's Chicago to the cornfields and cow pastures of Richmond, Illinois, "Population 300."

As dramatic a shift as this was, I quickly adapted, reveling in rolling hills and long gravel roads where play came with a breadth and width found only in country surrounds. My father continued his job in Chicago, which meant trips back were frequent enough, and, particularly after my grandfather died, my grandmother visited often.

When she did, it was like a rock star descended.

It was her exoticness, so disparate from anything in our whitewashed midwestern town, that fueled the fandom. Our assemblage of friends, with their paler bloodlines and predilections for the mundane, found her both peculiar and fascinating. She had a thick Greek accent, a voluminous bosom that commandeered her entire torso (something that, as a child, I found structurally confusing), and her style of dress was darkly Mediterranean. But it was the food she concocted that proved her greatest currency.

Our appetite for it was insatiable, which triggered all manner of maternal jealousy. While we salivated over freshly baked bread and pecan caramel rolls made with real butter, my very mid-century mother insisted Imperial Margarine was just fine and, really, "Weren't the rolls a bit dry?" Perfectly roasted leg of lamb with mint jelly was appreciated but, perhaps "tough and slightly gamey." Exquisite cheese and apple strudel (no frozen phyllo for my grandmother) was acknowledged as delicious, but maybe "a little greasy."

We children, however, would have none of it. In the tumultuous, demanding life of our growing family, in our beige little farm town of northern Illinois, Grandma was the Queen and her visits to us, and ours to her, were unforgettable highlights.

Then they stopped. She stopped coming; we stopped going. We didn't know why, but questions were met only with obfuscation, fomenting the conviction that my mother and grandmother simply couldn't exist in the same world together. We had no doubt my father was a willing colluder in this banishment, which only stoked our anger and confusion. Why would he ostracize his own mother, the only grandmother we had?

Implied was that she'd said something untoward about or to my mother, something nefarious enough to tip whatever scales teetered from earlier infractions. But with no answers available, we were forced to get on without her. The distractions of childhood initially made that possible, but as I got older, and the duration of her exile stretched into my college years, the metastasizing tension of our fractured family was palatable.

On Christmas break my freshman year at the University of Illinois, I sat tucked in the backseat of the car as my father and mother drove me home for the holidays. Making our way on snowy highways north, we neared the turn toward Chicago, and I was struck by an irrepressible thought.

"We should go see Grandma." I said it. Out loud.

My mother stirred. She looked left to my father, who remained concentrated on the road ahead. He had no discernable reaction. But I would not be deterred.

"It's Christmas. I want to see her It's been long enough."

I don't remember feeling brave; I only remember missing my grandmother. I don't remember exact words; I only remember the sense that a chord had been struck, one that rang with both guilt and relief. My mother softened, my father relented, and we made our way to Victoria Street.

While they stood at the bottom of the steps, I knocked. My grandmother opened the door and looked at me with stark incredulity. Tears seemed to burst from her eyes as she pulled me to that pillowy bosom, holding me as if it had been as many years as it had. I cried too. Even my parents cried.

She was my Christmas gift to my brothers and sisters.

From there, and with no explanation, my grandmother was suddenly back in the fold . . . just as I was leaving it. The next years were filled less with home and more with finding my own way. My family had now grown to include an eleventh child, a sister seventeen years my junior, and the charged mix of aging parents and too many people in too small a space propelled my permanent exit. I hit the road with a rock band and ultimately ended up in the City of Angels, where I got on with the business of growing up, defining my career, curating my friendships, and falling in and out of love. Time with my grandmother dwindled in the distance.

My relationship with my parents also became an ephemeral thing of brief conversations and few trips back. They were occupied with family, and I was immersed in the hand-to-mouth existence of a rocker with a waitress job. When I met a charming British ex-pat who brought romance and a little luxury into my life, he fell enough in love with me to suggest travelling back for a visit and introductions.

Again, it was Christmas, that perennial holiday of reunions and rapprochements, and my charming Brit charmed them all, especially my grandmother. When he pulled her to the dance floor during a raucous family gathering, the tiny, top-heavy, seventy-eight-year-old Greek woman set her ever-present purse down and bounced up like a giggling schoolgirl. He had her at, "Shall we dance?" and her delight was memorable.

But while he was bewitching her and gaining the general acceptance of my family, I was withholding the fact that he and I were now living together. The omission was intended to preserve the gaiety of the season but would soon prove portentous to the health and welfare of my relationship with my father.

As a fierce and committed Catholic (something I'd long previous abjured, and, likely, had never truly been), my father's views were filtered, always, through the prism of dogma. There was no parsing, no gray area, and certainly my living with a man without the benefit of marriage was non-negotiable. So after my Brit and I returned to Los Angeles and it was no longer feasible to hide our cohabitation, I framed the reveal by appending that we planned to be married "at some point." This was not necessarily true, but we *had* referenced it once or twice, and somehow I thought the qualification would soften the blow. It did not.

On my birthday that March, instead of the usual card, I got a letter from my father written in parable form: a third-person narrative about a misguided girl who came to the decadent city to find her fortune only to be seduced by corruption and debauchery, leading to her drug-addled death in the puddle of a dank urban gutter. Happy Birthday. The End.

I was incensed. As a dedicated young woman paying my own way, pursuing my career with verve, never once imbibing in drugs of any kind, this narrative was so off beam as to snap whatever thin thread remained between my parents and me. I called home and when my mother answered, I lit into her like a woman on fire.

My rebuttal was absent any buffer, and as she begged me to wait to talk to my father when he got home, I howled, "If he is that unaware of who I really am, I no longer consider him my father!" I officially removed myself from the family roster. She was sobbing as I hung up, but I was unmoved, my hurt that profound.

Many months passed with no further contact. My walls were up. Theirs walls were up. But finally, deep into the experiment of our separation, my father called and left a message:

"We're traveling west in the RV, staying at a KOA park near Los Angeles. We'd like to see you." He made clear they would not be visiting my home, but, rather, expected me to come out to the park. This was not a winning strategy. I did not respond.

Not long after, and purportedly unaware of the extended family's westward itinerary, my grandmother called about her own trip to Los Angeles. She asked to stay with me, in my "debauched" abode (not her words, just my sarcastic thoughts), and I felt such gratitude for her acceptance, her unwillingness to judge, that I welcomed her with open arms.

But an ironic twist was at play. The (ultimately *not* so charming) Brit and I were no more, but—too chagrined to share this humbling information with my parents, at least not yet—I irrationally continued the charade of my sinful status. Not wanting to burden my grandmother with facts she couldn't divulge, I chose to maintain my well-meaning chicanery. I told her the Brit would be out of town.

Despite her genuine disappointment, I convinced her I would be sufficiently entertaining on my own, and she and I did it up like two girls gone wild. I'd never had her to myself before, certainly not as an adult, and this was treasured time. On her third night there, after a run through Hollywood and a lovely dinner out, we arrived home to a message from my father:

"We'll be at the park on Friday." He left directions. I fumed.

"He won't come here because I'm a sinner, but I should go there for him?"

"Not for him, for your brothers and sisters."

"So he gets to win either way!" My wail was remarkably adolescent.

"It's not about winning; it's about your family. They want to see you."

"Why are you taking his side?"

"I'm taking *your* side . . . you'll feel bad if you don't go. We'll both go. I'll make strudel."

As if that declaration closed the deal, she started up the stairs to bed. It struck me, then, that her stance might be reflective of her own stonewall of years earlier, a missed wedding that was likely a regret.

"Fine!" I snapped, "But if he starts lecturing about the Bible and my wicked ways—"

She turned with twinkling eyes. "We'll take the strudel and leave."

That *did* close the deal.

On Friday, we packed our carefully wrapped confection and headed off to a KOA park far enough from the city that time and traffic gave free rein to my anxiety. My grandmother stared silently out the window, her purse on her lap like a security blanket, and I wondered if my trepidation was contagious.

But when we pulled into the park and saw my brothers and sisters wrapped around a picnic table waiting, I knew she'd been right. They scrambled to the car as if I were the prodigal sibling, a metaphor my father would likely have appreciated. As they marched the trays of precious booty inside, admonished to wait until dinner to pounce, my grandmother and I cautiously entered the RV.

My mother gave me a hug and kiss; brushed my hair aside affectionately, clearly set on ignoring whatever might be in the middle of the living room. But as my father rose to hug his own mother, his eyes met mine and the look was inscrutable. He gave me a cursory hug, then sat talking to his mother. I waited briefly, but when no attention was forthcoming, went out to join my siblings.

The afternoon was spent in campground activities and commiseration about the state of family affairs, particularly this tumultuous road trip. They were, each and every one, furious at the decision to circumvent my home, but remained as powerless as I to change the mind of our intractable father.

Dinner on the patio was muted and uneventful, filled with small talk and deflective chatter. As cleanup commenced, and my parents and grandmother went inside to wrap and wash, I stubbornly stayed behind, refusing the intimacy of the small space inside. When it was time to go, I sent a brother in to roust my passenger. My mother carried out the now empty strudel trays, placed them in the trunk, and came to me with tearful hugs. I hugged her back . . . and meant it.

Finally my grandmother made her careful exit down the RV steps, and we said our rounds of protracted goodbyes and climbed into the car. As I pulled down the drive toward the freeway, she looked at me and, with the slightest edge, queried:

"You don't say goodbye to your father?"

"He didn't have much to say to me; what would be the point?"

She sat for a moment, then suddenly shrieked, "Stop!" Alarmed, I slammed on the brakes. She began frantically looking around, under her feet, and across the backseat. "Ack, I left my purse in there!" I hadn't noticed, but she was, indeed, without her ever-present accessory.

"Really, Grandma? You left your purse in there? Are you kidding me with that?"

As sincerely as a bad actress could, she responded, "I was flustered saying goodbye; I must have left it on the table."

I felt a surge of both rage and tenderness, fully aware of the ruse. But what choice did I have? She needed her purse; the clan had already scampered off to whatever was happening at the community pool, and clearly I couldn't ask her to climb those rickety steps again.

With a roll of my eyes, I threw the car in reverse and backed up to the RV. I paused, hoping for reprieve, but she reached over and gave me a shove toward the door. Glaring, I hopped out, clamored up the steps, and swung the screen door open without a knock. My father looked up, startled to see me, and there was no denying the sheen of tears. I hesitated, uncertain about what, specifically, was behind his display of emotion.

"I . . . sorry . . . Grandma left her purse in here."

He pulled it from behind another chair and held it out to me. I had to walk closer to get it. When I did, he gently took my hand. I stiffened, not sure how to respond or what his touch meant.

"We're coming through the city in a couple of days." His voice was gruff. "Your brother found a place for lunch near your neighborhood. I was hoping you'd meet us there before we go."

"Dad . . . I—"

"We're still family," he said somberly. "You're still my daughter. We still love each other. Can't we find a compromise?"

He remained holding my hand and I didn't pull away. No apologies were yet forthcoming, but he was right: he was still my father, I was still his daughter, and, yes, we still loved each other. Beyond that, I couldn't say.

As my grandmother and I headed back, we talked about her trip home the following day and when I might see her next. She didn't ask what transpired inside the RV, and we didn't discuss her sweet, transparent ploy to save my floundering relationship with my father. We both understood the mechanics.

The next day, as she sat, tiny and tearful, in the backseat of the cab, I held her hand as if afraid to let go. She'd always been my champion, my defender; the person who accepted me for the wholeness of my heart, with no agenda, no inventory of demands. I was just her "little blondie," and she was simply the most exotic, complex, and unconditionally loving grandmother a girl could have. As the cab pulled away, and I watched her move farther and farther from my view, my own tears flowed.

That was the last time I saw her. She died on Christmas morning, standing at her oven removing a tray of buttery Koulourakia baked for the family holiday. Dropped by a heart attack, she left life doing what was surely her most singular gift: making food for the people she loved. I still have one of those cookies, wrapped and held in a little jewelry box like the treasure it is to me.

I did go to that lunch with my family. I sat next to my father, and we spoke guardedly of my work and the songs I was writing; he talked about places they'd been, where they'd stop on the journey home, even waxed eloquent about the jicama in his salad, something he'd never before tasted. We both knew harder discussions were needed but would be left for another time. As we sat in our version of the compromise he'd asked for, I felt the gentle push of my grandmother's hand urging me toward this delicate détente. And I smiled, thinking of an artfully forgotten purse and the small Greek woman who understood the bargaining power of love.

The End

To read about my grandmother's immigrant story in an essay I wrote with my sister, Mary Amandes, our family archivist, input the following link:

https://lorrainedevonwilke.substack.com/p/rescuing-debbie-an-immigrant-story

Photo courtesy of family archives.

LIKE A CHILD

a song of duty and dreams

THE MOTHER OF MY REINVENTION

A life began with good intentions
Pages blank to fill
Plans were made with strict attention
Much to be fulfilled

Childish dreams he put aside
Rules to be obeyed
Obligation, family's pride
Fortunes to be made

This is your life, his father said
Play out your hand
But who can I be, he wondered
If I sell my soul to be his kind of man?

CHORUS:
Oh, we take and we give but where is the rhyme
Or reason for this life we defend?
If we die and we live regretting the time we've lost
Then it's time to dream like a child again

His world grew large as he got smaller
Lost in all he'd found
But how can one man make a difference?
Walls are tumbling down
Tumbling down

BRIDGE
Once I had faith in what I believed as a child
That one single touch could save a life caught in the wild
Where did I leave the dreams I imagined were mine?
Can I be redeemed?
Please tell me my life hasn't run out of time

CHORUS
Oh, we take and we give but where is the rhyme
Or reason for this life we defend?
If we die and we live regretting the time we've lost
Then I wish to dream like a child again

Oh, we take and we give but where is the rhyme
Or reason for this life we defend?
If we die and we live regretting the time we've lost
Then it's time to dream like a child again

Two men in my life inspired this song: one strapped on a tie and suit coat and deftly abandoned his dreams for a corporate career. The other refused the assignment. I thought of them both as I wrote these lyrics.

Lyrics by Lorraine Devon Wilke; music by LDW & Rick M. Hirsch
Photo by Hunters Race

To enjoy a listen, input the following link:

https://soundcloud.com/lorraine-devon-wilke/like-a-child-by-lorraine-devon

LEGACY IS NOT JUST FOR THE FAMOUS

an essay

WHENEVER A CELEBRATED figure dies—whether an artist, an entertainer, a famed activist, or noble leader—we out here in the land of non-celebrity, and even some who share that vaunted status, speak much about the legacy of that person. We discuss their resume of beloved books, music, or films; we speak of their accomplishments in making the world a better place, their contributions to humanity, the simple pleasures they brought to those who indulged in all they had to offer. We honor them by our attention to, and appreciation of, what they left behind. Their bequest. Their legacy.

Yet, oddly, we seem to ascribe the concept of *legacy* only to those of renown. We rarely use that term about the uncelebrated, the non-famous, the everyday folks unknown beyond their smaller circles. They are, or were, after all, just "regular people," certainly not meritorious enough to bear the burden of legacy, right?

I don't think so. In fact, I think the misassignation of "legacy" as a remnant only of the famous and celebrated has done a grave disservice to our human race of people living all kinds of lives, large or small. It has deflected our understanding of, and excused our inattentiveness to, what's expected of each and every one of us in our short time here on earth: leaving it better off than we found it.

"But who expects that of me? I'm just a regular person. Nobody cares what I leave behind, what I do or say. Nobody will remember me beyond my family. Nobody pays attention to if I contribute or what I contribute. I'm not obligated to the world. I'm just trying to survive, and as long as I take care of my family, keep my kids from going off the rails, don't kill anybody, maybe have a little fun before it's over, that's good enough for me."

Those statements were actually said to me, and they do illustrate a common train of thought. Which is understandable. Not everyone wants to get all "grand" about how they choose to live their lives. They don't necessarily want to think that big, extend their views so globally, burden themselves with a higher purpose that might demand more awareness of the consequences and reverberating effects of their actions.

If that paragraph of denials is the totality of what you think on the subject, then you might have misunderstood the definition of legacy. The fact is, whether you're thinking about it or not, value it or not, are celebrated or not, your legacy *is* being created, either consciously or unconsciously, with or without your curation, by everything you do. Why would you abdicate ownership of that? Don't you *want* some involvement in how you're remembered, what those you touch think of you or how they frame your life? What effects are left in your wake?

Frankly, I've come to believe that ignoring the task of legacy (or allowing it to formulate without your conscious thought) has contributed greatly (or not so greatly, as it were) to the weakened striving for and inarguable demeaning of what have long been considered desirable human traits: integrity, compassion, humanity, generosity, honor, and open-mindedness. When words like "woke" are snarled as denigrations of those traits, we've lost the script.

Maybe it's that too many presume they're invisible enough to *not* be held responsible for their actions. Or they subscribe to elements of the current era that celebrate the *opposite* of those traits, thinking nothing of the negativity they engender, the ugliness they inject into their sphere. Empathy is dismissed at "weakness," compassion is not even considered; some care so little about "making the world a better place," or "living an admirable life," they pillage and plunder with a sense of entitlement, in some cases, glee.

It's in evidence daily, as we're bombarded (often from the current leader of the land) by social media with incomprehensible levels of vitriol and ignorance that sometimes have lasting and powerful repercussions. Untold hordes engage in thoughtless, destructive exchanges as if "no one's watching," or normalize hacking, "deep faking," and now, AI deception, in a world of zero privacy. They forget that screenshots can immortalize deleted threads, emails are never really lost, and hateful speech and knee-jerk reactions may later be regretted, the fallout sometimes irrevocable. So they spend precious hours of life sharing hateful dialogue and trolling those who might not share their beliefs. They bully and attack with little concern for who they hurt or what negativity they foment. They steal art, denigrate kinder people, and make any online interaction a brutal gauntlet.

And they do all this with impunity, because they're either hiding behind a screen name, they're convinced they won't be found out; they think they're above reproach, or they simply don't care. They don't care if their persona, their name, their identity, the essence of who they are is attached to something heinous and hideous. They don't care about legacy. They likely consider that "woke," too.

But they should care.

Whatever you might believe about spiritual life, life beyond the physical realm; the existence of energy and consciousness, the fact remains that what we create has impact. On us, our families and friends, the communities in which we live, the countries to which we pledge our allegiance; the global alliance we call the human race. It doesn't matter if you're famous, notorious, large, small, or in-between, you have impact. Visible, not visible, felt, not felt; ignored, denied, or dismissed . . . *you have impact.* That's your legacy. Even if you're someone who doesn't give a damn what that impact is, the way you affect and influence your children, your personal circle, the world at large, anything and everything you touch, *is your legacy.* You *should* care about that.

Because there can be no purpose in life more important than making one's imprint something of value. We may not be able to control whether we succeed, gain fame and fortune, or become the kind of person whose death inspires Facebook posts, but that can't be the criteria. The criteria for any person's legacy are simply this:

Make everything you say, do, write, create, share, influence, or affect be something your children, your mother, your father, your spouse, the people you care most about—*YOU*—would be unequivocally proud of. Do no harm. Control your anger, your hate, and the urge to damage or demean. Embrace the simplest of rules: "do unto others." Stoke empathy at every turn by considering how your words and actions would feel *to you* . . . then act accordingly.

If nothing else, *do* think about if you *were* famous and people were talking about you after you died. What would they say? What would they celebrate? How would you be remembered?

Morbid, maybe. But sometimes we have to jar ourselves into understanding more clearly the impact we do have. Little things add up, good and bad, and what you leave behind really ought to be something meaningful, something of value.

The thesaurus offers one synonym for "legacy" that I particularly like: *gift.* My mother taught me that one always leaves a gift when one is a guest somewhere. And given the brief, transitory nature of life, I'd suggest we are all guests on this planet, in our lives, in every moment we live . . . hence, gifts should be left. Which confirms my thesis:

Your legacy is your gift. Think about the gifts you leave behind.

Photo by LDW

MAKING HERSELF KNOWN

a short story

TODAY WAS THE day she would figure it out.

That had been the plan since she rolled out of bed at 6:43 am, ate her cinnamon Pop-Tart, perused her bookmarked media sites, and settled into her routine.

Except there was no routine.

Prudie Kayfall had managed to get to her fifties with little marking her life beyond a recently dead husband, two grown kids in distant states, and a job at the local pharmacy that required little more than showing up and running a cash register. This being her day off, she decided it would be the day she figured out what to do with the rest of her largely invisible life, which appeared to be carrying on despite her ennui and despair.

"You've got all the time in the world now that Dad's gone, but still you sit around moping about the emptiness of your life." Her son, Jonathan, the older of her children, was not the diplomatic sort. "Go *do* something, Mother!"

Regional manager of a men's clothing line specializing in fitness apparel, Jonathan was a go-getter who'd happily leapt across the country to grab his brass ring, and was currently making high-six-figures, dating a model, and "not planning to have children." Prudie found him frequently condescending, occasionally as cruel as his father, and ruthlessly ambitious in ways that confused her. How she and her dead husband had raised such a child when neither of them had been go-getters—or even knew the language of go-getting, particularly the ruthless kind—was beyond her. But, however he'd arrived at his current self, Jonathan got under her skin like no other (at least since his father died), bombarding her with lectures and life coach platitudes that frequently pressured her into actually following his directives.

Like his most recent, to avail herself of, "It's Time to Be the YOU *You* Want To Be," an online course conducted by a previously unknown woman named Betsy whose TED Talk on becoming the "*ME I wanted to be*" went viral. Prudie reluctantly signed on, mostly to assuage Jonathan, but the first session succeeded only in clarifying that she didn't want to be any of what she'd been so far with no idea of what *her* to be next.

"Was there something you imagined for yourself that you haven't yet had the opportunity to pursue?" Betsy gently prodded during the "participation" round.

Yes, Prudie thought, *feeling happy, cherished, and seen.*

Out loud she blurted, "I wanted to be famous," with immediate regret. It was a ludicrous thought to put into form, but it *was* a thought that had flitted through her mind from time to time, inspired by an article on Katherine Hepburn in which the iconic star stated that her earliest ambition was, "to be famous." That unabashed declaration was thrilling to consider because it came without any mention of, "at what?" Prudie, who decided that fame could potentially be a remedy to her ongoing state of invisibility, had never sorted out the "at what?" either (though clearly, and ultimately, Katherine had).

"Okay ..." Betsy continued, "but have you given any thought as to how you might achieve that goal?" She was being patient; others in the online gallery appeared less so, displaying visible signs of twitchiness (a woman in the upper right-hand corner surreptitiously rolled her eyes). Prudie felt twitchy herself but decided to analyze the question.

"I was the assistant editor of my high school literary magazine my senior year. I thought about trying to be a writer."

"Excellent!" Betsy smiled as if she'd just won something. "Now take *trying* out of the equation and let's just *do*." She gave Prudie a raft of mantras and affirmations with instructions to, "spend time writing down your thoughts, ideas, and imaginings" in hope of inspiring subsequent action. With a tight-lipped, "thank you," Prudie clicked out of the session (she didn't particularly care what the other women—they were all women—aspired to), deciding she wasn't going to do any of what Betsy suggested or even attend the remaining sessions. As she moved to the couch with a box of Wheat Thins, she also decided she wasn't going to sign up for any further workshops regardless of Jonathan's admonishments or disapprovals.

Still, as she got to the bottom of the cracker box and licked the salty remains from her fingers, she started daydreaming about what might happen if she *did* do all those things Betsy suggested and actually came up with an idea for a book, miraculously garnering fame as a successful writer. What a lovely dream! She leaned back to picture it: writers' conferences, bookstores with wide-eyed fans coveting her autograph; traveling the country for book clubs and media events.

Then reality struck and the spark blew out.

Real writers had something to say; something they were compelled to convey in literary form. She had none of that. Nothing to say, to write about, to share with eager readers. Maybe she had no imagination; was that possible? She certainly hadn't had much experience with it up till now. But somehow she instinctively knew the problem wasn't lack of imagination; it was the smallness of her life. The smallness of *her*. She was completely uninteresting. Her mind was uninteresting. Even her daydreams were uninteresting. Her dead husband used to say she fit her name:

"Prudence. That's so you. A prude. Conservative, careful, flat, boring." He sometimes said this to her after sex.

It never mattered that, as she'd recounted to him more than once, she'd been named after Prudence Courteney, the "delightful but unfortunate heroine of Evelyn Waugh's novel, *Black Mischief*," a book her late, literary-obsessed mother loved. He just saw it as another way to cleverly (so he thought) squash her spirit, a task in which he frequently engaged, along with making sure she knew she was unattractive, untalented, and largely unnoticeable.

She was glad he was dead. Sometimes she wished he'd died sooner but realized that was an evil thought to admit to.

"Fame seems like a rather strange goal for you," her daughter, Kelly, remarked during their phone call later that night. "I get that it might seem fun from the outside, but, Mom, why would you want to be famous at this stage of your life? I don't get it." Kelly was generally kinder than Jonathan but just as clueless to her mother's aching, empty soul. She'd relocated to the opposite coast to follow her husband's burgeoning career as a bio-researcher in the marine sciences, where she taught middle-school, rescued dogs, and was currently raising a daughter, aged five. She was happy, loved, and settled, making Prudie's kerfuffled state as foreign to her as running a cash register at a pharmacy. "I don't mean to be cruel, Mom, but what, really, could *you* possibly do to become famous?"

But it felt cruel, her question, certainly the emphasis on *you*, but of course it was also the elephant in the living room, as her dead husband used to say (usually in joking reference to Prudie's "heft"). "Yes. I know; I currently do nothing that would warrant fame . . . or even anybody's notice. Maybe that's the problem: I'm an invisible person, as I have been most of my life, and maybe I've finally had—"

"You have never been invisible to me!" Kelly fiercely rejoined.

Prudie was touched. That might be true. Kelly had always been a kind and loving child. "Thank you, sweetheart, that's very nice. But the fact is, you're states away; Jonathan rarely calls, and I spent three decades with a man who never failed to find me unworthy of notice. Now that he's gone, I've started to think maybe he was right in his small-minded little asshole way. So when I think about what my personal contribution to the world might be before I'm dead and buried, there's been an urge lately to shuck off that shitty identity and make myself known."

There was a beat of silence.

"Wow." Kelly was rendered momentarily speechless by Prudie's highly unusual outburst. "I'm not sure how to respond. I didn't know that about Dad; that's awful and I'm sorry he made you feel that way. But, Mom, even if I understand your reasoning, I still don't see how you could possibly get famous at this point of your life." She actually sounded sad having to say that.

It made Prudie sad too, the cutting truthfulness of it, so she quickly changed the subject and ended the call on the sweet note of her granddaughter's chirping, "Bye, bye, Grandma!"

But what remained was the emptiness. The fact that her life was bereft of any personal dimension that could pull her out of obscurity, much less make her famous. She knew in her heart of hearts it was a stupid goal, but she honestly thought that when her husband died, taking with him all his mockery and contempt, she'd blossom like a flower, with new thoughts, new ideas; new aspirations. But it seemed, after so many years of being battered by that mockery and contempt, she lacked the emotional muscle for such transformation.

The alert for her daily blood pressure meds snapped her from her doldrums, and as she crossed to the kitchen, she was surprised to notice that, for some reason today, the typical resentments stirred by any thought of that dead husband had taken a turn. By the time she'd swallowed her pills and recycled the Wheat Thins box, that turn took form.

Defiance.

"Fuck 'em all," she said out loud. Fuck her dead husband. Fuck her condescending son, her incredulous daughter. Fuck that eye-rolling woman in the upper right-hand corner of the Zoom gallery. She *could* be a writer; she *could* get famous. She just needed to figure out how to perk her perspective, broaden her scope, fire up her brand. Notable, life-changing things needed to happen, completely unlike anything anyone in her family might imagine her doing, particularly her dead husband. That, in fact, was a prerequisite.

Now she was excited.

Over the next week she spent large chunks of time on various incognito pages of her browser researching possibilities, giving herself permission to push against boundaries; rub the edge of the envelope, all the clichéd things one does when trying to invent the most outrageous version of themselves. Most of what she perused was wildly out of her wheelhouse, some of it criminal, a lot potentially terrifying, but desperate to shatter the smallness of her life, she rationalized that the sheer excticness of any resulting chaos could provide useful literary fodder.

Remembering E.L. James, another chubby, former housewife who skyrocketed to viral fame after writing the *Fifty Shades* books, and with the encouragement of her much younger friend and pharmacy workmate, Yolanda, she (very) briefly considered the heretofore unimaginable avenue of porn. She wasn't clear in what capacity—doing it, observing it, then writing about it? —but the absurd suggestion emanated from Yolanda's recent forays into what she described as "fun little sexcapades" with her latest boyfriend, Titus. Their romps involved the video feature on her smartphone, lots of reportedly "ferocious sex" in Yolanda's condo guest bedroom, and a contact list of Titus's many libidinous friends. The seediness of it all barely registered with Yolanda, who was thrilled by the attention, but Prudie, already squeamish around her friend's overt flaunting of impossibly deep cleavage and a fondness for random butt-patting, could only look away when offered "a peek" of said videos. She was amazed at Yolanda's sexual appetite, but ultimately decided that she, herself—besides finding it all too wet and creepy—was too old, too fat, and not sexually bold enough to venture down that path. As her dead husband never failed to point out, sex for her had always been a thing of dimmed lights and furtive sheet action. Nothing worth chronicling in any of that.

So, what else? What sharp turn in her road could inspire a memoir? She gave brief thought to "drug running," a rather dramatic term chortled by another work colleague who was selling "excess and therefore unmissable" pharmaceuticals to friends and family and had suggested a collaboration. There was money to be made, she was assured, which was always nice, and certainly there was something buzzy about mimicking elements of the *Weeds* narrative. She conjured up gritty scenarios of dark corners, misguided decisions, and heroic rehab dramas, then considered that any first-person perspective would require that she be either the addict or the criminal. Since she couldn't handle liquor much less drugs, and fear of legal intervention shattered any romance with the outlaw life, the idea was quickly deemed a non-starter.

Next, coffee with a neighbor in her building led to tales of this woman's "selective shoplifting," and how her adventures were going viral due to giddy Tik Tok posts about her "process." This light-fingered gal claimed to have surreptitiously returned all the items lifted and given that "it's so fun!" she wondered if Prudie would want to "play the game with her just for kicks." Prudie found she couldn't fling off her basic moral core and, frankly, had already decided illegal concepts were off the table.

Another dead-end.

As time went on and she continued exploring other extreme options for viral-worthy literary capers, she became confused and overwhelmed, caught between wanting to be wild and realizing she just wasn't born to be. Maybe her dead husband was right; she *was* just flat, careful, and prudish. "Quirky without flair or charm," he once put it. One can't go viral with that brand.

Deciding to pause her pursuit, she was home on a Thursday night watching whatever reality show her remote had landed on when Yolanda texted:

A bunch of us R at Lucky's. The band SMOKES. Come over!!! xoxoxoxo

Seriously? We have work tomorrow!

Sandy's birthday!!! Fuck work! <3 <3 <3

Prudie was about to text, "*2 tired*," when it struck her that maybe this was exactly what she needed to do more of: GO OUT. That was simple enough, wasn't it? Be amongst people. Interact. *You won't get more interesting sitting around here watching the Housewives.* Join the fray; see if it leads somewhere interesting. Probably not, but still ...

As she later sat alone at a sticky table nursing her now-flat rum and coke (her first and last), watching Yolanda flail on the dance floor for what seemed the tenth song in a row, she decided that her overall lack of social activity had misguided her into thinking *this* activity would be fun. It wasn't. It was loud and boring, and as she'd skipped dinner to make it happen, she was now starving and annoyed. She turned toward the bar and noticed a posted menu.

That's what she'd do; she'd sit at the bar, order a burger, and enjoy it without the distraction of Yolanda's energetic jabbering every time she stopped at the table to sip her drink. The only open spot, however, was next to a rather large man in khakis and a plaid shirt who, once she sat down, kept glancing her way, which she found off-putting. After she placed her order, assiduously avoiding any turn in this fellow's direction, he spoke up.

"I just had one of their burgers . . . a high recommendation."

"Glad to hear it," she mumbled, continuing to stare straight ahead at the bar mirror through which she could see his smile was, admittedly, benign and quite friendly. Still, his uninvited encroachment was vexing.

"I'm sorry . . . what?" He leaned in, apparently not catching her mumble.

She suddenly turned to him, eyes flaring, and barked, "I am *not* going to sleep with you, asshole!"

He jerked back as if punched. "Wow! Well, that's good because I'm not going to sleep with *you* either!"

Her face flamed as she stared down at her napkin, stunned by the volatility of her response, especially considering she was not the kind of woman who typically inspired lust from strange men sitting at bars. Or any men, for that matter.

Shaking his head, the poor guy tidied up his area as if readying to leave. "Damn, the world is strange." He glared at her as he stood up. "What gave you the idea I was angling for that anyway? Not only is it rude and presumptuous, but I'm here with someone. I was just being friendly, for God's sake!"

She hadn't noticed a woman anywhere near but was too embarrassed to make the point (and what point would there be in making that observation anyway?). She finally turned to him, expression chastened. "I'm sorry. Really, I am. I don't know why I said that. It *was* rude and presumptuous. I'm a fairly recent widow and never go to bars, so clearly I have no idea how to act around people in general but men in particular. If we could just write it off to that, I'd appreciate it." Her face was so red she appeared sunburnt.

Empathy appeared to wash over him as he sat back down. "I'm sorry for the loss of your husband—"

"I'm not." Apparently blurting out inappropriate things was going to continue a bit longer.

"Okay . . . well ..." He had no idea how to respond to that. "I'm sorry you're feeling uncomfortable in here and, yes, we can write it off to that."

"Thank you. My name is Prudie . . . which at this point you probably think suits me just fine."

He yelped a laugh. "Hah, that's a good one! Nice to meet you, Prudie. I'm Scott." He didn't reach out his hand, clearly wary of crossing any further boundaries.

At that moment her burger was delivered and as she turned to eat, a very scrawny, pale man—who looked to be about a hundred years old—wobbled up and tapped Scott's shoulder, gesturing with his head toward the bartender.

"Another one?" Scott asked him.

The man nodded. As Scott placed the order, the man turned his rheumy eyes toward Prudie, though she wasn't sure he actually saw her as he didn't smile or seem to make eye contact.

Scott handed him his beer. "Game still going?"

He nodded.

"Okay, I've got about fifteen minutes before I need to leave, so go wrap it up."

As the man shuffled back to the dart area, Scott gave Prudie a chagrined smile. "Sorry I didn't introduce you. He had a stroke last year and is non-verbal at this point. But, oddly, even though his eyesight sucks, he can still throw a mean dart for some reason. It's his one physical activity so I like to give him as much time as possible."

Prudie wasn't sure she needed that much detail into the lives of these strangers, but felt some obligation to be nice—pleasant, at least—given her verbal assault of moments earlier.

"He's your father?" she asked, continuing her meal.

"Yes ... Buddy."

"You live together?"

"No, he's in a care facility not too far from here. I get him out every Thursday; comes to rehearsals with me, then we stop by here afterwards. He's big on darts and has a pal here who plays with him, so it's the highlight of his week."

The word "rehearsals" piqued her interest, especially since Scott, with his soft, pudgy body and unremarkable face, did not appear to be the kind of person who'd be engaged in activity that required rehearsals. Which she knew was a stereotype and not very kind, given her own comparable traits, but still.

"You're in a play?" she asked, tamping down her incredulity for the sake of continued decorum.

"No, a choir."

Again, surprising. "Oh, you sing?"

He grinned. "Well, good enough, I guess. It's a unique kind of choir."

"A church thing?"

"No, it's all very secular." He stood up and pulled on his jacket. "It's a volunteer group called HeartSing Choir ... we sing in hospices and nursing homes, sometimes ICU wards."

"Wow. That must get sort of crowded."

He laughed. "It's just three or four singers at any given time; we participate in rotation. And it's very quiet singing, very gentle—hard to do for a big boomer like me. Anyway, it's beautiful stuff and very comforting, I'm sure, for the people listening."

"I bet—" Before she could complete her sentence they were again interrupted by Buddy, who'd quietly reapproached.

"Ready to go, Dad?" Scott asked.

Buddy nodded.

"By the way, Dad, this is Prudie. We just met tonight, and she seems like a pretty nice lady." He smiled in Prudie's direction; she felt decidedly undeserving of that generous assessment.

"Nice to meet you, Buddy," she replied.

Buddy nodded, again without eye contact. Scott shrugged apologetically and reached into his coat pocket.

"Listen, if you'd ever like to come to a choir rehearsal, see what it's about, you could give me a call—"

"Oh, I don't think that's something I'd be interested in," she quickly remarked, not wanting to give him any invitation whatsoever to be in touch with her.

"No problem." He left his card on the bar. "But my number's there if you change your mind. And maybe I'll see you in here again, yeah?"

"Probably not." She left it at that.

He appeared taken aback by her conviction but smiled as the two men turned for the door.

At that moment a very drunk Yolanda approached. "Whasssup, girl? You over here flirting your butt off without me around to coach your ass? And, hey, where's your boy goin'—"

Prudie rolled her eyes, popped off her stool, and patted Yolanda's head. Going to the table to grab her coat, she realized there was no mystery as to why she struggled finding something exciting to do with her life when she could barely tolerate minor human interaction in an average dive bar. She sighed, and with a quick wave to Yolanda, already back on the dance floor, she fled home.

Time, as it is wont to do, carried onward, bereft of further clues as to how to make herself known, and despite relentless calls from her children querying, "What are you doing this week to improve your life?" Three months had passed since the truncated, "It's Time to Be the YOU *You* Want To Be," and she felt no closer to her stated goals, whether finding something to write about, becoming a viral sensation, or in any way getting closer to finding fame. In fact, she'd actually retracted since the night at Lucky's. She could almost hear her dead husband sneering.

As her Friday shift at the pharmacy came to a close, she went to the breakroom where Yolanda sat plunked in a chair digging through her purse. "Hey, some of us are going to grab dinner downtown; wanna come?"

She didn't. But she should. She needed to eat. She would know everyone there. She had nothing else on her schedule. It was Friday night. She should—

"Oh, look, I forgot I had this." Yolanda held out a battered business card covered in purse dust and remnants of what looked like blush. "That guy you were talking to at Lucky's? He left this for you. You didn't pick it up, but I did ... in case, you know, you changed your mind." She grinned lasciviously and shoved it into Prudie's hand. "He looked like a sweetie to me."

Prudie closed her fist around the card, reducing it to a wad, and begged off dinner. She suddenly felt sad—was it mention of the guy she'd so handily rebuffed? —and didn't want to deal with Yolanda's relentless perkiness. She'd grab a sandwich from the deli next door and find a movie to stream.

As she sat at her dining room table staring at the crumbled card now spread open in front of her, she wondered what she should do with it. Wondered why it wasn't already at the bottom of her trash bin. She thought about people volunteering to do something quiet and gentle, as Scott had described it, for people who likely couldn't respond in any appreciable way. No reviews on Yelp or social media, no rounds of applause, no standing ovations. Who knows; maybe they couldn't even hear it. But nonetheless, people showed up every Thursday to practice singing gently and quietly for dying, dire people, just to ... well, she wasn't sure why.

Which made her think about Scott's invitation to attend a rehearsal. Maybe she should. Just to listen and watch for the sake of observing, of figuring out what the singers got out of it; of having a new experience. She, herself, wasn't much of a singer; shower warbles and car sing-alongs, but no real talent. Her dead husband once put his hands over his ears feigning aural pain when she belted out the chorus of a favorite song on the radio. He'd snorted, "You could call hogs with that barker," and she stopped singing whenever he was around. Actually, she stopped singing all together.

Scott was as surprised to hear from her as she was to call, but he didn't ask why she was suddenly interested, which she appreciated. He texted the address of the community center where they rehearsed, and she said she'd come by "one of these Thursdays." It wasn't until a couple weeks later she showed up.

Deeply uncomfortable and almost childishly shy, she entered the room to be greeted by a jovial woman wearing the nametag, "Sheila," who introduced herself as the musical director. Scott waved from the front of the room where several people were pulling chairs into a circle. She noticed Buddy sitting in the audience area a few rows away. Sheila, who was very pleasant, suggested that Prudie sit, "anywhere you like and just enjoy the singing." Scott beamed like a proud host as he sat down with the assembled singers.

Prudie chose a seat a few rows back from Buddy's; they were the only two observing the goings-on. She noticed a reclining chair in the middle of the singers' circle abutted by three small stools and wondered what that was all about. After a few announcements, Sheila conducted vocal warm-ups, then called out the first song. There was what seemed a singular breath, then the entire group came in on the beginning note as if psychically in sync. The first round was sung in unison, a lilting melody with poetic lyrics like, "we surround you with love," and after that round, Sheila made a motion with her hand, and they split into harmonies.

That was when Prudie felt herself gasp. The sound of those voices, those harmonies, soft, gentle, and so incredibly, heartbreakingly beautiful, raised goosebumps on her skin. She closed her eyes, leaning back in her chair as if transported somewhere—she didn't know where, but somewhere ethereal and exquisite. When the song ended (it was very short) she sat up and glanced around, hoping her reaction had gone unnoticed. It had, thank God, as surely she would have looked like a swooning idiot.

But as the rehearsal continued, those emotional tugs persisted, even triggering the inexplicable urge to cry (which she managed to stifle). It was strange to her how moving it all was, how hypnotic. At one point Sheila stood up and pulled the empty reclining chair in the middle of the circle into a flat position, asking who'd like to "play the patient." She turned to Prudie to explain: "Since we sing to people lying in beds, it's good for the singers to practice with a stand-in ... or lie-in, as it were." She smiled; the others smiled; it was clearly a well-worn joke. Scott looked over at his father.

"Hey, Dad, want to play patient again tonight?"

Buddy leaned forward, then rose and slowly shuffled over to be helped into the recliner. Scott and two other singers sat on the three short stools at the recliner, and within seconds began ever-so-gently singing the chosen song, their eyes laser focused on Buddy. Again, it was quite beautiful.

When the song concluded, there was quiet discussion with Sheila and the others about how well the harmonies had blended, if everyone was comfortable with the hand signals; how that particular song felt to all of them. Prudie watched with fascination, noting that Buddy appeared as if he'd fallen asleep. When Scott touched his shoulder, the old man slowly opened his eyes, but before he could get up, Sheila intervened.

"Actually, Buddy, would you be willing to do one more round? We have to wrap up a little early tonight—another group rented the room without realizing we were here—so how about we stick with this formation just to save some time?" Buddy lay back without hesitation. Sheila looked at the singers. "I know we don't usually do this either, but I was thinking—since we have a new guest here tonight—why don't we end with an old standard Prudie could sing with us." She smiled in Prudie's direction. "Would you like to join us for the last song?"

Prudie immediately blanched. "Oh, no, that's okay," she demurred. "I'm not a singer ... probably wouldn't know the song anyway."

"Do you know Amazing Grace?"

Of course she did. Everyone knew Amazing Grace. "Yes, but

I've been told I could call hogs with my voice."

That got a laugh from everyone, but Sheila was not to be deterred. "I highly doubt that, Prudie, and, frankly, you don't need to be a great singer. You just need to share a bit of your heart and sing softly. It's all about the intention to express love and compassion. I have no doubt any friend of Scott's and Buddy's has the capacity for that."

Buddy's eyes remained closed, but Scott smiled at her from across the circle. Prudie was confused as to why these people were being so accommodating, so sweet and lovely. She wondered if it was some kind of trick, some conceit. Were they manipulating her to join? Was she being flattered to make a donation? Was it a cult?

It didn't feel that way. It felt like they simply wanted her to join them in a song. Though flushed with awkwardness, she got up and made her way to the circle. Sheila started the song and, as the group blended gentle harmonies, she slowly joined in.

It felt clumsy at first, singing out loud in the presence of strangers, but her voice, however soft, sounded clear and on pitch. At least she thought it did; it seemed to match the other voices. She then wondered if it had always been clear and on pitch, even when she sang around her dead husband. Wouldn't that be something?

By the time they got to the second verse, she stopped thinking about him, stopped thinking at all, and with eyes closed, sang as if no one had ever shut her up or made her feel invisible; ever called her names or laughed at her joy; ever insulted her exuberance, sneered at her spirit, or dismissed her as dull and inconsequential. It was cathartic and exhilarating, this singing, and she let it wash over her like a balm.

When the song ended, there was a breath of silence. Prudie's eyes popped open to see faces turned toward hers and she panicked. Had she been too loud? Battered them with dissonance? Her cheeks burned beet red, but everyone only nodded, their approval clear.

"I had a feeling you were a heart singer," Sheila said, obviously pleased with her experiment.

Prudie couldn't help but smile. "That felt ... nice."

Buddy's eyes suddenly opened, and he turned slowly in Prudie's direction, making direct eye contact with her for the first time. Then, unexpectedly, in a voice made husky from his many months of silence, he softly croaked, "You must be an angel. I heard the voice of an angel." He reached for her hand and squeezed it, then leaned back and once again fell silent as everyone looked at each other, stunned and delighted by his utterance.

Scott's face was lit up as he helped Buddy out of the chair. Walking past Prudie, his arm firmly around his frail father, he leaned down and whispered in her ear, "He hasn't spoken in over a year. Not a word. You *must* be an angel."

Shaken to be the focus of this tender moment, Prudie felt tears again gathering and worked hard to keep them from tripping down her cheeks. The rest of the group continued buzzing about Buddy as they scuttled around reassembling the room, calling out goodbyes as they left, one by one. By the time Prudie had her purse and coat, the place was almost empty, the other group waiting outside. Sheila thanked her for coming and asked if she'd consider joining. Prudie smiled and said she'd think about it, "But probably not; I have too much going on right now."

She didn't. She had nothing going on. It was just a rote, knee-jerk response to any entreaty that requested her involvement, likely why she'd also turned down Scott's invitation to join him and Buddy at their post-rehearsal trip to Lucky's. Or wouldn't call Angela back to catch her up with, "What happened at the dead people choir?" Or hadn't answered Kelly's email wondering how the search for relevance was going.

But as she walked to her car and drove slowly home, she couldn't help acknowledging that something inside her had shifted, lifted, tonight. She wasn't sure what. It felt so fleeting, so ephemeral; she didn't know how to define it, how to articulate it to herself, much less to anyone else. She was afraid the overpowering feeling of euphoria would dissipate. And she didn't want it to. She wanted to hold onto it, that feeling. It felt transcendental, magical even, and she knew it had happened in that minuscule moment when Buddy's eyes peered into hers and he called her an "angel." He *saw* her. He saw *her*. Even for just a moment. He identified her as someone good, someone of value; someone who'd made him shake off his own limitations and speak after so long a silence.

It was a tiny thing but so big, this feeling she'd never had before, that it both shook and exhilarated her. It said she wasn't invisible. It said her dead husband was wrong about her. It said she didn't need to go viral or get famous or make porn or write a book. It said she was fine just as she was.

Later that night she deleted all the sites she'd bookmarked under, "interesting viral opportunities," trashed the folder on her desktop titled, "good writing ideas" (there was *one* good idea she saved); she ran a "find" on every document on which she'd written the words, "how to get famous," and got rid of them all, then called Scott to ask how she went about signing up for HeartSing Choir. He conveyed how happy he was that she decided to join, suggesting he and Buddy pick her up next Thursday "as a welcome gesture!" She said she'd drive herself but appreciated the offer. Which she honestly did.

Lastly, she texted both her son and daughter to tell them she was done with her misguided quest, as she'd come to realize she was fine just as she was. She informed them that she'd now be singing quiet songs to the sick and dying, and that felt to be as good and special a thing as any person could do. When they later texted back, expressing incredulity about what led to this "rather random decision" (Jonathan's words; Kelly was less prickly), she simply replied that pursuing the goal of fame (which she'd always known was absurd) was no longer needed. She'd already been discovered. She'd opened her mouth and closed her eyes and forgot the hurt and sang a song and touched a soul who felt her worth and told her so.

She'd made herself known.

The End

I love Prudie. She's not based on anyone I know but she came to me one night so real and alive with all her edges and twitches that I wanted to give her a story. A story to make her... well . . . known*!*

Photo by Jessica Da Rosa

DROWNING

a song of loneliness and heartache

A little lost, maybe a little scared
With a smile that could hide a million tears
A pretty face shadowed by little bits of promise
That have all but disappeared

Another drink, maybe a fumbled kiss
From a stranger she thinks she needs to know
A need so strong for a soul so weak…he leads
She knows that she will follow

He takes her in his house, he takes her in his arms
He takes whatever he might need
He loves her some but not nearly enough
To keep her heart from bleeding, she cries

CHORUS:
Somebody give me an anchor, somebody throw me a line
Somebody tell me to breathe, I just might drown this time
Oh I think I'm drowning this time … drowning

Just a week, maybe a little longer
She's sure he never meant to stay away
But when her Mama cried she knew she'd never be stronger
Than the shattered little girl he left that day

Now so alone sometimes she loses perspective
Of who she is, what part of her is real
So if somebody touches her for even just a moment
It's a moment…she gets to feel

Maybe this one will be the one to stay
The one who see behind her eyes
But when he leaves without ever noticing
She reaches out to emptiness and cries

CHORUS
Somebody give me an anchor
Somebody throw me a line
Somebody tell me to breathe
I just might drown this time
Oh I think I'm drowning this time

BRIDGE
Every morning she wipes away the shame
She swallows any taste of sorrow
But every night she's back to play the game
So sure tonight he'll see tomorrow
(*please stay . . . just stay*)

CHORUS
Somebody give me an anchor
Somebody throw me a line
Somebody tell me to breathe
I just might drown this time

Somebody give me a reason to believe
Maybe there's something that's mine
Someone to pull me to safety
I'll just drown this time
Oh I think I'm drowning this time … drowning
I might be drowning this time … drowning
I think I'm drowning this time . . . drowning

"Drowning" has an interesting link to the new mayor of NYC: While trying to find the lyrical story of this song, I happened to watch a movie called Hysterical Blindness *starring Uma Thurman. About a thirty-something woman abandoned as a child by her father and now desperately floundering to find love, the ache and loneliness of Uma's character so moved me that when I finally sat down to finish the song, the lyrics just poured out, an homage of sorts to that story. Turns out Mira Nair directed that film. Turns out she's also Zohran Mamdani's mother. Interesting, I thought.*

Lyrics by Lorraine Devon Wilke, Music by LDW & Rick M. Hirsch

Photo by Jimmy Johnson

To enjoy a listen, input the following link:

https://soundcloud.com/lorraine-devon-wilke/drowning-by-lorraine-devon

DESPITE TRENDS TO THE CONTRARY, KINDNESS MATTERS

an essay

WHAT IS LEFT of the world when wicked men have their way, and indoctrinated followers raise voices and fists to further a message of hate and fear?

What is left of the world when relentless war and death are met with greed, ambition, and despotism, shunting aside concerns for life and liberty, mothers and children, this group or that?

What is left of a world when lies become lexicon, corruption becomes the norm, and weak people propagandize to weaker people who capitulate to believing both the lies and corruption?

What is left of the world?

Kindness. Goodness. Truth. Empathy. Compassion.

All are still there, existing between the corroded lines of gaslighting screeds, violent bigotry, lethal ICE tactics, and blind fealty to demagogues, pushing up like hearty stalks that split cement, vibrant and robust despite impediment. There are, in fact, and despite media fixation on the contrary, so many good, kind people in the world that we *can* have faith in ideals of change, peace, and progress. It's the smoke and mirrors of a chaotic world that play tricks on us, wraps us in scrims of hate and fear, myopia and regression. Those who perpetuate that chaos have deigned empathy a weakness, compassion as "woke"; concern for the greater good a waste of bandwidth.

But they're wrong; they're liars and cheats, bigots and xenophobes, so they *would* try to convince you otherwise. Don't believe them, whether media, politicians, opinion leaders, or your mouthy neighbor next door who just hung a MAGA flag in their front yard.

There's debate over whether Donald Trump created, inspired, triggered, or simply ushered in the very worst amongst us, but whatever spin is true, that "worst" is here now, seated at the table to which he invited them, embedded in our government, attacking protesters, murdering mothers, violating persons of color, caging immigrant children, militarizing cities, stealing tax dollars, corrupting government agencies, tearing down the White House, doing the bidding of despots, taking over countries, and otherwise toxifying the American experiment.

As experiments go, this one could use a tweak.

Watching duly elected senators and representatives, members of our very own United States Congress, snark, snarl, and name-call on Twitter/X like snotty twelve-year-olds convinced of their own cleverness makes clear just how sophomoric even the supposed *best* amongst us can get. Listening to hordes of the indoctrinated screeching back lies they've been fed about elections, vaccines, crowd numbers, ballrooms, deadly shoots, and bad actors makes clear just how dangerous cultism can be. Observing daily diatribes of right-wing media spewing utter nonsense in fealty to a person so corrupt even corrupt people are in awe reminds us of how corrosive media can be when allowed to.

Yet still …

In the midst of that madness, luckily in numbers that outnumber *them*, are the millions of kind people, good people; people who care enough about their fellow humans to do the right things. Stand up to ICE. Work long hours to care for the sick and elderly. Teach and mentor children. Administer schools, create beautiful things, research important advances, and promote environmental improvements. People who run for government because they actually want to make life better for their constituents rather than use it to enrich and aggrandize themselves, their families, and their cronies. People who are passionate about creating racial equity in our divided society, who see immigrants as essential members of our diverse landscape; people who listen and speak with consideration, respect, and civility. People who refuse to reject truth to further lies and self-serving agendas.

These people outnumber *them*.

Yet in a society where clickbait rules and madness get the attention, we spend so much time reading about, listening to, recoiling at; analyzing, reacting, and responding to the despicable, heinous words and deeds of the worst people we've sickened ourselves, literally and figuratively. We're immersed in it, overwhelmed by it, to the point that it's almost impossible to believe that good people, kind people, honest people actually exist. We don't hear much about them; they're not as interesting, it seems; they don't inspire as many clicks and read-throughs. Studies have been done to support that fact.

And, sadly, that won't likely change. Our culture is too entrenched in the trend of tabloid titillation. Train wrecks, car crashes, murder conspiracies, and sex scandals will always garner more curiosity amongst those for whom news is entertainment.

No, the only way to inject balance into the equation is to not only *be* that kind, good person, but to share and engage with those who also fit the description. Make a pact to not only rant, rail, and act against injustice, dishonesty, and corruption, but to also shine as much light as possible on the kind people, the good people, the honest, productive, life-changing, planet-saving, uplifting, integrity-inspiring people who vastly outnumber the worst amongst us who *do* get the headlines. Let's make our own headlines for something other than notoriety and scandal.

In fact, let's make *kindness* trend. We've had enough of the other and it's just about killed us. It's past time to invite kindness to the table. It might be hard to believe during this trying time that kindness can find its way to the door, but I am, nevertheless, holding a seat.

Photo by Matt Collamer

THE WARMTH OF THOSE FEW WORDS

a very short story

I'M IN LINE at the post office. It's moving slowly, as it always does, and I wonder why they don't just open another window, as I always do. People-watching in an effort to quell my twitching impatience, I notice a woman ahead of me with a young girl, about four, I'd guess. I assumes it's her daughter, given the warmth between them, and I can't help but gaze at the sweet tableau they make as they chat and giggle with each other. At one point, the mother lifts the tired child up to sit on the empty counter they abut, and in a tender moment that makes my heart clutch, the girl tucks into her mother's shoulder, burrowing her head against her neck. When her eyes catch mine, she smiles with the soft confidence that all is right in her world.

I look away, an unexpected lump in my throat. I check my watch and note that six minutes have lapsed with little progress, and I'm suddenly angry. I sigh loudly. Twice. A few people turn, most, it seems, in commiseration; one, on a phone, frowns as if I'd disturbed her. The woman and child seem not to notice.

Then it strikes me, what I'm feeling. It's grief. Yes, I'm peeved at the glacial pace of this line, but the sweet image in front of me has hit like a gut-punch, a reminder that my own once-needing-and-hugging child is no longer around to need or hug. He's off soaring into his future, and his absence, after a lifetime of presence, has left a chasm. Yes, he's doing what he should be doing; yes, it's well past time to reconcile with that reality, and yes, I have, but as I watch this ever-so-ordinary moment between a mother and daughter, I want to sit down on the grubby floor of this post office and weep.

Can you imagine, when even a sigh triggered annoyance from Phone Lady?

So, no, I won't make a fool of myself. I'll swallow this unexpected sorrow, check emails, and hope I get out of here before my meter expires. As I pull out my phone, a text buzzes:

'Mom, gf tried meatloaf last night--seriously heinous. Told her yours was killer-- send recipe!! luvU ❤ "

I feel a flush of something lovely. Apparently I am still needed.

For meatloaf. Whatever. I'm warmed by those few words. I respond with a thumbs-up, a quick message about "when I get home," and an echoing heart.

When a newly arrived postal worker finally opens an additional window and the line surges ahead, the lady on the phone turns to look at me as if expecting my applause.

Still smiling, I almost give it to her.

The End

Not my story—my son never had a girlfriend who tried to make meatloaf—but the moment in the post office? That was real. Ah ... letting go.

Photo courtesy of family archives.

WISDOM BRIDGE

a song of questions and ponderings

Sit down, I gotta ask you something
I hope that you are feeling wise
I gotta know, do you know the way to go
To find my piece of paradise?

I'm a woman of substance, I'm a woman of means
But what does that mean in the course of a lifetime?
They say that on another shore lies happiness
But tell me, is the river wide?

CHORUS:
Meet me on Wisdom Bridge
Maybe we can both decide
Whether to walk a while in the same sweet mile
Or cross onto the other side

So many people looking for themselves
Don't know who they're looking for
So many answers and questions and "help-yourselves"
They find the key but lock the door

It's a painful persuasion
The urgency of ticking time
But a master of fate knows the moment we wait
Can lead us to our peace of mind

CHORUS:
Meet me on Wisdom Bridge
Maybe we can both decide
Whether to walk a while in the same sweet mile
Or cross on to the other side

Meet me on Wisdom Bridge
Maybe we already know
If there is more to learn then the bridge won't burn
If we wait a little while to go

SPOKEN BRIDGE
Hey, I'm just sittin' here trying to figure something out
Why don't you come over and give me some of your perspective?
'Cause, you see, I seem to be at a turning point
And I don't know what to do
Do I move onto something new?
Or just live for a while where I stand ... what do you think?

CHORUS:
Oh, I'm standing here on Wisdom Bridge
Oh, on Wisdom Bridge
Can we talk a little while?
I need to walk another mile

Oh, Wisdom Bridge
Standing here on Wisdom Bridge ...

Written as a paean to the freedom found in sometimes not *making a decision, allowing more of life to reveal itself before you do, "Wisdom Bridge" was originally recorded for the soundtrack of the film,* To Cross the Rubicon, *and is currently a vibrant entry on the setlist of my band, Sixth & Third.*

Lyrics by Lorraine Devon Wilke, Music by LDW & David Resnik
Image by StockSnap

To enjoy a listen, input the following link:

https://soundcloud.com/lorraine-devon-wilke/wisdom-bridge

THE MOTHER OF MY REINVENTION

reflections on a mother

TUCKED IN HER lift chair, chilled and uneasy, she waits for tea and dry toast to calm her daily quarrel with queasiness. Hunger. Thirst. With raised eyebrow and a sardonic grin, she remarks, "It ain't easy gettin' old." I commiserate, but she dismisses my empathy; tells me I'm too young to understand. I don't bother to correct her.

She's tired, though she's been in bed since breakfast. It's a long day by two o'clock, and not necessarily a good one. Though there *are* good ones: days when she plays cards, sings along with glee, or attends video Mass in the community room. She still relishes her three squares and always brightens at the sight of chocolate. She's now in a wheelchair full-time but loves a roll around the park. She's almost eighty-five, a widow for fifteen years, and a diagnosed Alzheimer's patient for five.

She is my mother.

I left home—and her—a long time ago. I left hard and fast, no quibbling or weepy boomeranging. My mother refers to this as, "when you ran away," which isn't far from the truth. It had been a challenging childhood.

I am a third child, the third girl in a family of eleven children. My two older sisters and I, by virtue of gender and birth order, became "little mommies" for smaller, younger siblings while we were still smaller, younger siblings ourselves. And though being in charge of an infant at six-years-old is, perhaps, too steep a learning curve, the responsibility *did* promote skills found useful in later life. I not only learned to change diapers, feed babies, and wrangle toddlers, I became adept at making meals, doing laundry, and running interference for a mercurial and confounding mother at the same time. And that was before I got to high school.

By the time I *did* get to high school, I was bone-weary of family and desperate to fly. Somewhere. Anywhere. Graduation couldn't come quick enough and my departure for college was so swift high school friends claim I never even said good-bye. I don't remember; I was moving too fast. I came home the summer after freshman year, but by the next, I was gone for good. My first apartment was a hideous ninety-dollar-a-month single with lousy furniture and a stuttering landlady, but it may as well have been heaven.

It wasn't just the weight of trading too much childhood for "little mommy-hood." It wasn't just the burden of my parents' religion with its restrictive views of human interaction (i.e., boys and sex). It wasn't even that one-on-one time in a big family was too spare to be satisfying. It was that I couldn't find an honest way to consistently and compassionately tolerate my mother.

She was a paradox. One minute clever and creative, the next enraged and irrational. She was impossible to predict and easy to trigger. She loved music, did a mean jitterbug, and had a wildly romantic relationship with the handsome man who was my father. She could make any day a holiday, taught us that fun was our birthright, and, oh, she loved with a passion. All this provided the good that pushed against the other. Her dark side. The turbulent state that came with frenzied tears, cold silences, or rages that scattered us like terrified animals.

As a child, I would tremble at the sound of her stomping downstairs to mete out punishments I could never seem to avoid. She would be physical, vocal, and unrelenting, and when control snapped and life got the best of her, everyone suffered.

She tried; I believe she sincerely tried, but she was undeniably overwhelmed by a family too large to manage, a husband often too detached to meet her emotional needs, and a psyche too fragile to offer the flexibility and endurance required by the job.

So when I left, I stayed away and kept her away. She and my father didn't meet my husband until years after we eloped, and I'd already given birth to a son. They were that distant and I was that intractable.

But life is surprising. You grow older and live longer, tripping on expectations not met or the sharp pangs of disappointment and heartache, and you learn some things. You learn that not all dreams come true, not all promises are kept. Life humbles and sometimes softens you. You accrue compassion for things you might not have previously understood, and that expands your view.

It wasn't until years after I became a parent that I saw my mother beyond the filter of a child's eye. When I attached to my own child, learned the frustrations, passions, and struggles of parenting, I gained perspective on what she'd experienced, many times over, in her own role as a mother. When my marriage met challenges or I felt distanced by a distant husband, I understood her anguish at the hands of her own husband's penchant for the same. Simply put, I began to see the human behind *the mother*. And I had empathy.

She is a third child herself; a brother and sister preceded her. Her mother died shortly after her birth, and her father abandoned all three to be raised by her mother's extended Irish family, who loved, took good care, and kept kegs flowing in the dining room. She claims it was a happy life—I'm sure much of it was—but when my father died many years after that childhood, she wailed that she'd been "abandoned" by all the men in her life, asking through tears how a father could leave his children without a look back. I had no answer for her. But it seems, regardless of her rosy, revisionist narrative, she'd suffered for it all.

She suffered for growing up without the intimacy and guidance of a mother's love, or the constancy of a father's. She suffered for the raging alcoholism in her family. She suffered for being an orphan whose need for love could hardly be filled. And now I, as an adult, mother, wife, and family survivor myself, was beginning to understand her story. It made me ache for her. It made my heart open.

Countless people I know are caring, or have cared, for aging parents. It's a rite of passage and a task like no other, requiring a depth of dedication I'd rarely felt for my mother prior and wasn't sure I could conjure into being now. But ten years after my father died, my aging, rudderless mother was in need.

Her short-term memory was slipping away, and she was often sick and in pain. Incapable of caring for herself responsibly, the family was running out of options. We needed a new plan, and all eyes were on me. "Look away!" a voice hollered inside my head. "You don't have to take it on. You left a lifetime ago for good reason; it's not your job!" That voice was loud, but its mantra rang hollow. Because I could see, as clear as the day I left home, that after other siblings had done their part, it *was* my turn to take it on. It *was* my job.

So I leapt, all-in. No turning back, no quibbling, no lack of conviction. Mother was coming to town. With the collaboration of my brilliant and indispensable brother, and our network of family and friends, I was going to participate in the care and feeding of the woman I'd fled so many years ago.

And so the Tour began.

But let's be clear: I'm not a saint. Far from it. Some days I suck at the job. I wake up and feel my teeth grinding, resentful that I have to leave yet another unreturned message for her doctor, or rifle through reams of paperwork to get thorny insurance issues worked out. I don't want to drive over to her facility to have the same conversation over and over or play that infernal card game again. I sometimes feel real anger that I'm expected to schedule my life around her myriad doctor appointments, am required at meetings I didn't expect, or obligated to "run right out" to pick up items she's lost or broken. I cringe when I see the name of the facility on my caller ID, wondering if she's been taken to the hospital, is being ornery with the night staff, or... God forbid... *that* call. And, yes, I sometimes feel, once again, like a "little mommy," only this time the child I'm caring for is my mother. The irony is inescapable.

But there is another side to this: an awareness of some sprouting evolution, hers and mine. In her case, the dementia creeping into her personality has done a curious thing. It's stripped away her anger and narcissism. It's pared her down to the purest, most basic essence of who she is. A human being who can be grateful and appreciative, smile even through pain, or tell me how happy she is to see me walk through a door. A woman who can genuinely thank a son for dinner out, or a daughter-in-law for laundry in. Who can find delight with grandsons who make her laugh or interview her for class projects. A person who can listen to and make note of someone in front of her, even if she can't remember who they are or what they just had to say.

This is different woman. A different mother. And this different mother is allowing me to be a different daughter.

I look through photographs of her from time-to-time to remind myself that she was once as vibrant and appealing as any young girl finding her way in the world. She had sexy legs, a smashing sense of style, and an infectious grin. She was flirtatious and sought after, ultimately loved by a man who found her beautiful and exciting. She could laugh raucously and make others laugh as loud. I study those photographs and say to myself: "She was young once, just as you were. And you will become old, just as she is. We're all in this together."

And so my mother and I continue our Mutual Reinvention Tour. I have found patience; she's become humble. I'm learning empathy, while gratitude is her new skill. We're both evolving, transforming; that can't be denied.

She looked at me recently and whispered, "I'm scared." When I asked why, she said, "Because I've made so many mistakes in my life, especially with you kids." She was concerned that, at the Gates of Heaven, she would be harshly judged, but mostly she wanted me to know she loved us all and was sorry for those mistakes.

I felt a tug. I'd been angry at her for so much of my life, the candor and vulnerability of the moment struck me. I took her hand and said, "Don't worry, Mom. If you're truly sorry, you've already been forgiven."

And as I said it, I realized that, like St. Peter at the Gates and God in the Heavens, I, her third daughter, her runaway, her lost child, had forgiven her as well. And in the swirling eddy of emotions that accompanied that revelation, sweet and simple love could be found.

Precious and timely, as the Tour continues.

Addendum: On June 8, 2020, in the midst of Covid lockdown, my mother died. We celebrated her life in August of 2022, bringing the Tour to its bittersweet, but meaningful, conclusion.

Originally penned in 2015, THE MOTHER OF MY REINVENTION was awarded as a Finalist in the Rocky Coast Writing Contest sponsored by The Maine Review and was published in their magazine that same year.

Photo courtesy of family archives.

A 'CHICK SINGER' REFLECTS ON DREAMS, HEARTACHE & RENEGOTIATION

an essay

A GIRL WHOSE name I don't remember had turned around. She was in the descending row on the choir stand in front of me, and apparently I was singing directly into her ear. With an expression bearing some harmonic of surprise, she said, "You have a really good voice," and I was equally surprised to hear those words. I sang loud and often, yes, but never before had any assessment of "really good" been assigned. That portentous comment opened my mind. I felt it, let it wash over me, recognizing the truth that singing not only transported me out of my everyday reality, but felt to be an honest, true talent.

And there it was. My designated dream. I was to be a singer.

It started with folk music, graduated to musicals, veered into singer/songwriter, but it was swiftly determined that I would set the world on fire as a rock & roll star. Not just a singer. Not just a rock & roller. No, I would be a "star." It was fated. It was my destiny. Everyone in my orbit bolstered that belief, which was powerful, propulsive stuff.

The wild and wooly '80s became the launch pad. With the requisite big hair, ripped fishnets, belts and bangles, my band DEVON became an LA success story with incredible gigs, recordings, management, financiers, and fans; interest, excitement, and conviction followed, then came panic, despair, and, ultimately, the cold-water dip of having exhausted the decade of both time and opportunities with no shiny record deal to show for it.

Oh, dastardly, dogged dream …

I was gutted. Empty, lost, and heartbroken. It was not a matter of just moving on; every aspect of my identity was wrapped up in that persona, that expectation, that plan. I *had* no other plan, no contingency. Despite my father's admonition to, "have something to fall back on," I'd been so convinced of my dream's fruition that "falling back" was a form of blasphemy. It would take hard grief, good therapy, and the love of excellent people to pull me out of the abyss.

But I did pull out. I survived. I recalibrated. I dipped into various other skill sets—acting, screenwriting, political opinionating, more music (though not of the "angling for stardom" kind, just … singing)—and began negotiating with my dream. Could I reinvent myself? Reconfigure, reimagine a path forward that felt authentic, real, and still offered some measure of my previous exhilaration? We haggled, my dream and I, and ultimately decided to keep music on a burner (if in the back), but let my photography and, particularly, my writing muses step forward.

I started a blog in 2010 when blogging was all the rage. Wrote for *HuffPost* for seven years. Got a fine art photography business going online. Then I started a novel. *A novel.* Crazy. Something I'd have never imagined doing prior. *After the Sucker Punch* was published in 2014, followed in 2015 by *Hysterical Love.* In 2019, a small publishing company, She Writes Press, took on what would be my most controversial novel, *The Alchemy of Noise*, and in April of 2025 my fourth, *Chick Singer*, was released by Sibylline Press.

There's something full circle about *Chick Singer* coming out at this particular moment of my life. A moment when I've acknowledged, as the group I've intermittently sang with over the last few years struggles to find time to convene, that I do, indeed, miss being in an active, working band. One that plays enough to feed that part of me that rode my bike down the street belting out rock tunes. Writing *Chick Singer* (which is not my particular story but one I certainly understand) allowed me to excavate much of what I'd experienced in losing, and letting go of, that musical dream of mine. It dug into the emotional, even spiritual, journey of finding (clawing?) your way back to some version of yourself that's healthy and resilient.

It was cathartic, in a way, writing that "chick singer's" story. It reminded me that dreams are not intransigent, immovable. Despite the reality that what one imagines for their life doesn't always evolve as planned, dreams have a way of adapting, adjusting, molding themselves into the *you* you ultimately become. Given my many years at it, I'm convinced they will doggedly stick with you until the end, though you may have to renegotiate from time to time.

But that's not a bad thing. I've learned they are very amenable to that, dreams.

Originally published in the June 2025 issue of Habitat2Art; reprinted in September 2025 in Bay City News.

Photo by Steve Sharp

RICHER FOR RAIN

a song of survival & triumph

THE MOTHER OF MY REINVENTION

Somebody told me that life
Is like a wheel, round and round
Sometimes you're giddy from riding the high
Sometimes your feet are flat on the ground
I was a girl with rich emotions
And a dream as big as the sky
So I set the wheel in motion
Convinced I would fly

CHORUS
Then somewhere on the way
I forgot my destiny
And I wasn't there to pray
When heartache knocked me to my knees
But then an old man touched my shoulder
He looked into the eye of my pain
He said, "Smile, girl, you are richer for rain"

So I packed up my wounds and my wisdom
Steeled for another run
Sometimes enchanted by fools and magicians
Wasn't sure what I'd become
Then I found a man who truly loved me
And a place to make my name
But when that gold ring swept above me
My hand slipped again

CHORUS
Then somewhere on the way
It seems that I lost track of time
And the young girl left one day
And took the dream I knew was mine
But then my lover touched my shoulder
He saw the hurt I couldn't explain
He said, "Smile, girl, you are richer for rain"

BRIDGE
I've got grown up angst and this young girl's heart
In a world that seems to believe that the art of life
Is best left in the hands of the young

But then somewhere on the way
I looked into the face of time
And what I found that day
Was more than what I left behind

And when I looked into the mirror
And saw the woman I became
I said, "Smile, girl, you are richer for rain"
You are richer for rain
You are richer for rain

Getting older can have particular sting when still chasing dreams in a youth-biased world. Still, we're all obligated to reconcile with that "circle of life," and as a feisty friend of mine once said, "Shut up and get on with it!" This song came to me as I was sitting at an outdoor table in the San Juan Islands, reveling in the good fortune of being in that beautiful place, in that moment, with people I loved. I was struck by the awareness that joy, happiness, and fulfillment can come in many forms, from many experiences, even the difficult ones we collect along the way, and whatever I might have missed, whatever I might have suffered, what I had was truly its own kind of wealth. "Richer for rain." Though the wheel is still in motion...

Lyrics by Lorraine Devon Wilke; music by LDW & Rick M. Hirsch
Photo by Jimmy Johnson

To listen, input the following link:

https://soundcloud.com/lorraine-devon-wilke/richer-for-rain-by-lorraine

The End

AUTHOR'S NOTE

If you're reading this note, odds are good you got to the end of the collection (*I'm delighted*), hopefully having experienced the various emotional moments intended. Thank you for reading.

If you'd enjoy exploring more of my essays and political/social introspections, I invite you to visit my Substack page, "Musings of a Creative Loudmouth," where I publish such things weekly. There you can grab a free or paid subscription and join in the many and myriad conversations we have there; I'd love to have you in the circle.

Lastly, should you also be interested in any of my longer works, those full-length novels I mentioned at the top, you'll find access links to all of them via my web address on the next page, and my Linktree will get you to everything I've got online, from books to Substack to YouTube to blogs to photos.

Feel free to get in touch. Know that I always appreciate your reading, enjoying, sharing, and reviewing my work.

TO CONNECT ONLINE WITH LORRAINE DEVON WILKE

Website:
www.lorrainedevonwilke.com

Social media, blogs & all other links via LinkTree:
https://linktr.ee/lorrainedevonwilke

Email contact @ info@lorrainedevonwilke.com

ABOUT THE AUTHOR

Born in Chicago, third oldest of eleven in a family that held creativity in high regard, Lorraine Devon Wilke was imbued with a love of music, art, theater, and books from the get-go. Folk groups in high school, a theater major at the University of Illinois, a writer of songs and prose, she hit the road with a rock & roll band and ultimately landed in Los Angeles where she's lived ever since. With music a persistent thread throughout, she immersed herself in acting, filmmaking, recording, and writing; started a blog in 2010, wrote for *HuffPost* and several other online sites, and in 2014 self-published her first novel, *After the Sucker Punch*; *Hysterical Love* followed in 2015. In 2019, She Writes Press released her third novel, the award-winning, *The Alchemy of Noise*, and in April 2025, Sibylline Press published her fourth, *Chick Singer.* Her fifth novel, *The Weight of Fables*, will be published by Sibylline Press in Fall 2027.

In the meantime, she's launched her popular Substack, "Musings of a Creative Loudmouth," sings with The Westside Threshold Choir, stays politically active with Sisters In Outrage, and spends precious time with family and friends, traveling, photographing the world, and playing gigs with her band, Sixth & Third.

www.ingramcontent.com/pod-product-compliance
Lightning Source LLC
Chambersburg PA
CBHW020011140726
47904CB00018B/2225

* 9 7 8 0 9 9 6 4 2 3 0 5 2 *